The Tales of the Heptameron

Volume I of V

The Tales of the Heptameron

Volume I of V

MARGARET,
QUEEN OF NAVARRE

Translated by
GEORGE SAINTSBURY

From the Authentic Text of M. le Roux de Lincy
with an Essay upon the Heptameron by the Translator

ÆGYPAN PRESS

The Tales of the Heptameron, Vol. I (of V)
A publication of
ÆGYPAN PRESS

www.aegypan.com

Table of Contents

The Heptameron

Appendix

Preface

The first printed version of the famous Tales of Margaret of Navarre, issued in Paris in the year 1558, under the title of "Histoires des Amans Fortunez," was extremely faulty and imperfect. It comprised but sixty-seven of the seventy-two tales written by the royal author, and the editor, Pierre Boaistuau, not merely changed the order of those narratives which he did print, but suppressed numerous passages in them, besides modifying much of Margaret's phraseology. A somewhat similar course was adopted by Claude Gruget, who, a year later, produced what claimed to be a complete version of the stories, to which he gave the general title of the *Heptameron*, a name they have ever since retained. Although he reinstated the majority of the tales in their proper sequence, he still suppressed several of them, and inserted others in their place, and also modified the Queen's language after the fashion set by Boaistuau. Despite its imperfections, however, Gruget's version was frequently reprinted down to the beginning of the eighteenth century, when it served as the basis of the numerous editions of the *Heptameron* in *beau langage*, as the French phrased it, which then began to make their appearance. It served, moreover, in the one or the other form, for the English and other translations of the work, and down to our own times was accepted as the standard version of the Queen of Navarre's celebrated tales. Although it was known that various contemporary MSS. were preserved at the French National Library in Paris, no attempt was made to compare Gruget's faulty version with the originals until the Société des Bibliophiles Français entrusted this delicate task to M. Le Roux de Lincy, whose labors led to some most valuable discoveries, enabling him to produce a really authentic version of Margaret's admired masterpiece, with the suppressed tales restored, the omitted passages reinstated, and the Queen's real language given for the first time in all its simple gracefulness.

It is from the authentic text furnished by M. Le Roux de Lincy that the present translation has been made, without the slightest suppression or abridgment. The work moreover contains all the more valuable notes to be found in the best French editions of the *Heptameron*, as well as numerous others from original sources, and includes a *résumé* of the various suggestions made by MM. Félix Frank, Le Roux de Lincy, Paul Lacroix, and A. de Montaiglon, towards the identification of the narrators of the stories, and the principal actors in them, with well-known personages of the time. An Essay on the *Heptameron* from the pen of Mr. George Saintsbury, M.A., and a Life of Queen Margaret, are also given, as well as the quaint Prefaces of the earlier French versions; and a complete bibliographical summary of the various editions which have issued from the press.

It may be supposed that numerous illustrated editions have been published of a work so celebrated as the *Heptameron*, which, besides furnishing scholars with a favorite subject for research and speculation, has, owing to its perennial freshness, delighted so many generations of readers. Such, however, is not the case. Only two fully illustrated editions claim the attention of connoisseurs. The first of these was published at Amsterdam in 1698, with designs by the Dutch artist, Roman de Hooge, whose talent has been much overrated. Today this edition is only valuable on account of its comparative rarity. Very different was the famous edition illustrated by Freudenberg, a Swiss artist — the friend of Boucher and of Greuze — which was published in parts at Berne in 1778-81, and which among amateurs has long commanded an almost prohibitive price.

The Full-page Illustrations to the present translation are printed from the actual copperplates engraved for the Berne edition by Longeuil, Halbou, and other eminent French artists of the eighteenth century, after the designs of S. Freudenberg. There are also the one hundred and fifty elaborate head and tail pieces executed for the Berne edition by Dunker, well known to connoisseurs as one of the principal engravers of the *Cabinet* of the Duke de Choiseul.

The Portrait of Queen Margaret placed as frontispiece to the present volume is from a crayon drawing by Clouet, preserved at the Bibliothèque Nationale, Paris.

ERNEST A. VIZETELLY
London,
1893

Explanation of the Initials Appended to the Notes

B.J. . . . . BIBLIOPHILE JACOB, I.E. PAUL LACROIX.
D. . . . . F. DILLAYE.
F.. . . . . FÉLIX FRANK.
L. . . . . LE ROUX DE LINCY.
M.. . . . . ANATOLE DE MONTAIGLON.
ED. . . . . E. A. VIZETELLY.

MARGARET OF ANGOULÊME,

QUEEN OF NAVARRE

I

Louise of Savoy; her marriage with the Count of Angouleme — Birth of her children Margaret and Francis — Their father's early death — Louise and her children at Amboise — Margaret's studies and her brother's pastimes — Marriage of Margaret with the Duke of Alençon — Her estrangement from her husband — Accession of Francis I — The Duke of Alençon at Marignano — Margaret's Court at Alençon — Her personal appearance — Her interest in the Reformation and her connection with Clément Marot — Lawsuit between Louise of Savoy and the Constable de Bourbon.

*I*n dealing with the life and work of Margaret of Angouleme* it is necessary at the outset to refer to the mother whose influence and companionship served so greatly to mold her daughter's career.

Louise of Savoy, daughter of Count Philip of Bresse, subsequently Duke of Savoy, was born at Le Pont d'Ain in 1477, and upon the death of her mother, Margaret de Bourbon, she married Charles d'Orléans, Count of Angoulême, to whom she brought the slender dowry of thirty-five thousand livres.† She was then but twelve years old, her husband being some twenty years her senior. He had been banished from the French Court for his participation in the insurrection of Brittany, and was living in straitened circumstances. Still, on either side the alliance was an honorable one. Louise belonged to a sovereign house, while the Count of Angoulême was a prince of the blood royal of France by virtue of his descent from King Charles V, his grandfather having been that monarch's second son, the notorious Duke Louis of Orleans,‡

---

* This Life of Margaret is based upon the memoir by M, Le Roux de Lincy prefixed to the edition of the *Heptameron* issued by the Société des Bibliophiles Français, but various errors have been rectified, and advantage has been taken of the researches of later biographers.

† The value of the Paris livre at this date was twenty sols, so that the amount would be equivalent to about £1400.

‡ This was the prince described by Brantôme as a "great débaucher of the ladies of

who was murdered in Paris in 1417 at the instigation of John the Bold of Burgundy.

Louise, who, although barely nubile, impatiently longed to become a mother, gave birth to her first child after four years of wedded life. "My daughter Margaret," she writes in the journal recording the principal events of her career, "was born in the year 1492, the eleventh day of April, at two o'clock in the morning; that is to say, the tenth day, fourteen hours and ten minutes, counting after the manner of the astronomers." This auspicious event took place at the Château of Angoulême, then a formidable and stately pile, of which nowadays there only remains a couple of towers, built in the fourteenth and fifteenth centuries. Soon afterwards Cognac became the Count of Angoulême's favorite place of residence, and it was there that Louise gave birth, on September 12th, 1494, to her second child, a son, who was christened Francis.

Louise's desires were now satisfied, but her happiness did not long remain complete. On January 1st, 1496, when she was but eighteen years old, she lost her amiable and accomplished husband, and forthwith retiring to her Château of Romorantin, she resolved to devote herself entirely to the education of her children. The Duke of Orleans, who, on the death of Charles VIII in 1498, succeeded to the throne as Louis XII, was appointed their guardian, and in 1499 he invited them and their mother to the royal Château of Amboise, where they remained for several years.

The education of Francis, who had become heir-presumptive to the throne, was conducted at Amboise by the Marshal de Gié, one of the King's favorites, whilst Margaret was entrusted to the care of a venerable lady, whom her panegyrist does not mention by name, but in whom he states all virtues were assembled.* This lady took care to regulate not only the acts but also the language of the young princess, who was provided with a tutor in the person of Robert Hurault, Baron of Auzay,

---

the Court, and invariably of the greatest among them." — *Vies des Dames galantes* (Disc. i.).

* Sainte-Marthe's *Oraison funèbre de la Royne de Navarre,* p. 22. Margaret's modern biographers state that this lady was Madame de Chastillon, but it is doubtful which Madame de Chastillon it was. The Rev. James Anderson assumes it was Louise de Montmorency, the mother of the Colignys, whilst Miss Freer asserts it was Anne de Chabannes de Damniartin, wife of James de Chastillon, killed in Italy in 1572. M. Franck has shown, in his edition of the *Heptameron,* that Anne de Chabannes died about 1505, and that James de Chastillon then married Blanche de Tournon. Possibly his first wife may have been Margaret's governess, but what is quite certain is that the second wife became her lady of honor, and that it is she who is alluded to in the *Heptameron.*

great archdeacon and abbot of St. Martin of Autun.* This divine instructed her in Latin and French literature, and also taught her Spanish and Italian, in which languages Brantôme asserts that she became proficient. "But albeit she knew how to speak good Spanish and good Italian," he says, "she always made use of her mother tongue for matters of moment; though when it was necessary to join in jesting and gallant conversation she showed that she was acquainted with more than her daily bread."†

Such was Margaret's craving for knowledge that she even wished to obtain instruction in Hebrew, and Paul Paradis, surnamed Le Canosse, a professor at the Royal College, gave her some lessons in it. Moreover, a rather obscure passage in the funeral oration which Sainte-Marthe devoted to her after her death, seemingly implies that she acquired from some of the most eminent men then flourishing the precepts of the philosophy of the ancients.

The journal kept by Louise of Savoy does not impart much information as to the style of life which she and her children led in their new abode, the palatial Château of Amboise, originally built by the Counts of Anjou, and fortified by Charles VII with the most formidable towers in France.‡

Numerous authorities state, however, that Margaret spent most of her time in study with her preceptors and in the devotional exercises which then had so large a place in the training of princesses. Still she was by no means indifferent to the pastimes in which her brother and his companions engaged. Gaston de Foix, the nephew of the King, William Gouffier, who became Admiral de Bonnivet, Philip Brion, Sieur de Chabot, Fleurange, "the young adventurer," Charles de Bourbon, Count of Montpensier, and Anne de Montmorency — two future Constables of France — surrounded the heir to the throne, with whom they practiced tennis, archery, and jousting, or played at soldiers pending the time when they were to wage war in earnest.[1]

Margaret was a frequent spectator of these pastimes, and took a keen interest in her brother's efforts whenever he was assailing or defending some miniature fortress or tilting at the ring. It would appear also that she was wont to play at chess with him; for we have it on high authority

---

* Odolant Desnos's *Mémoires historiques sur Alençon*, vol. ii.

† Brantôme's *Rodomontades espagnoles*, 18mo, 1740, vol. xii. p. 117.

‡ The Château of Amboise, now the private property of the Count de Paris, is said to occupy the site of a Roman fortress destroyed by the Normans and rebuilt by Foulques the Red of Anjou. When Francis I ascended the French throne he presented the barony of Amboise with its hundred and forty-six fiefs to his mother, Louise of Savoy.

[1] Fleurange's *Histoire des Choses mémorables advenues du Reigne de Louis XII et François I.*

that it is she and her brother who are represented, thus engaged, in a curious miniature preserved at the Bibliothèque Nationale in Paris.* In this design — executed by an unknown artist — only the back of Francis is to be seen, but a full view of Margaret is supplied; the personage standing behind her being Artus Gouffier, her own and her brother's governor.

Whatever time Margaret may have devoted to diversion, she was certainly a very studious child, for at fifteen years of age she already had the reputation of being highly accomplished. Shortly after her sixteenth birthday a great change took place in her life. On August 3rd, 1508, Louise of Savoy records in her journal that Francis "this day quitted Amboise to become a courtier, and left me all alone." Margaret accompanied her brother upon his entry into the world, the young couple repairing to Blois, where Louis XII had fixed his residence. There had previously been some unsuccessful negotiations in view of marrying Margaret to Prince Henry of England (Henry VIII), and at this period another husband was suggested in the person of Charles of Austria, Count of Flanders, and subsequently Emperor Charles V. Louis XII, however, had other views as regards the daughter of the Count of Angoulême, for he knew that if he himself died without male issue the throne would pass to Margaret's brother. Hence he decided to marry her to a prince of the royal house, Charles, Duke of Alençon.

This prince, born at Alençon on September 2nd, 1489, had been brought up at the Château of Mauves, in Le Perche, by his mother, the pious and charitable Margaret of Lorraine, who on losing her husband had resolved, like Louise of Savoy, to devote herself to the education of her children.†

It had originally been intended that her son Charles should marry Susan, daughter of the Duke and Duchess of Bourbon — the celebrated Peter and Anne de Beaujeu — but this match fell through owing to the death of Peter and the opposition of Anne, who preferred the young Count of Montpensier (afterwards Constable de Bourbon) as a son-in-law. A yet higher alliance then presented itself for Charles: it was proposed that he should marry Anne of Brittany, the widow of King Charles VIII, but she was many years his senior, and, moreover, to prevent the separation of Brittany from France, it had been stipulated that she should marry either her first husband's successor (Louis XII) or the heir-presumptive to the throne. Either course seemed impracti-

---

* Paulin Paris's *Manuscrits françois de la Bibliothèque du Roi*, &c., Paris, 1836, vol. i. pp. 279-281. The miniature in question is contained in MS. No. 6808: *Commentaire sur le Livre des Échecs amoureux et Archiloge Sophie.*

† Hilarion de Coste's *Vies et Éloges des Dames illustres*, vol. ii. p. 260.

cable, as the heir, Francis of Angoulême, was but a child, while the new King was already married to Jane, a daughter of Louis XI. Brittany seemed lost to France, when Louis XII, by promising the duchy of Valentinois to Cæsar Borgia, prevailed upon Pope Alexander VI to divorce him from his wife. He then married Anne of Brittany, while Charles of Alençon proceeded to perfect his knightly education, pending other matrimonial arrangements.

In 1507, when in his eighteenth year, he accompanied the army which the King led against the Genoese, and conducted himself bravely; displaying such courage, indeed, at the battle of Agnadel, gained over the Venetians — who were assailed after the submission of Genoa — that Louis XII bestowed upon him the Order of St. Michael. It was during this Italian expedition that his mother negotiated his marriage with Margaret of Angoulême. The alliance was openly countenanced by Louis XII, and the young Duke of Valois — as Francis of Angoulême was now called — readily acceded to it. Margaret brought with her a dowry of sixty thousand livres, payable in four installments, and Charles, who was on the point of attaining his twenty-first year, was declared a major and placed in possession of his estates.* The marriage was solemnized at Blois in October 1509.

Margaret did not find in her husband a mind comparable to her own. Differences of taste and temper brought about a certain amount of coolness, which did not, however, hinder the Duchess from fulfilling the duties of a faithful, submissive wife. In fact, although but little sympathy would appear to have existed between the Duke and Duchess of Alençon, their domestic differences have at least been singularly exaggerated.

During the first five years of her married life Margaret lived in somewhat retired style in her duchy of Alençon, while her husband took part in various expeditions, and was invested with important functions. In 1513 he fought in Picardy against the English and Imperialists, commanded by Henry VIII, being present at the famous "Battle of Spurs;" and early in 1514 he was appointed Lieutenant-General and Governor of Brittany. Margaret at this period was not only often separated from her husband, but she also saw little of her mother, who had retired to her duchy of Angoulême. Louise of Savoy, as mother of the heir-presumptive, was the object of the homage of all adroit and politic courtiers, but she had to behave with circumspection on account of the jealousy of the Queen, Anne of Brittany, whose daughters, Claude and Renée, were debarred by the Salic Law from inheriting the crown.

---

* Odolant Desnos's *Mémoires historiques sur Alençon*, vol. ii. p. 231

Louis XII wished to marry Claude to Francis of Angoulême, but Anne refusing her consent, it was only after her death, in 1514, that the marriage was solemnized.

It now seemed certain that Francis would in due course ascend the throne; but Louis XII abruptly contracted a third alliance, marrying Mary of England, the sister of Henry VIII. Louise of Savoy soon deemed it prudent to keep a watch on the conduct of this gay young Queen, and took up her residence at the Court in November 1514. Shortly afterwards Louis XII died of exhaustion, as many had foreseen, and the hopes of the Duchess of Angoulême were realized. She knew the full extent of her empire over her son, now Francis I, and felt both able and ready to exercise a like authority over the affairs of his kingdom.

The accession of Francis gave a more important position to Margaret and her husband. The latter was already one of the leading personages of the state, and new favors increased his power. He did not address the King as "Your Majesty," says Odolant Desnos, but styled him "Monseigneur" or "My Lord," and all the acts which he issued respecting his duchy of Alençon began with the preamble, "Charles, by the grace of God." Francis had scarcely become King than he turned his eyes upon Italy, and appointing his mother as Regent, he set out with a large army, a portion of which was commanded by the Duke of Alençon. At the battle of Marignano the troops of the latter formed the rearguard, and, on perceiving that the Swiss were preparing to surround the bulk of the French army, Charles marched against them, overthrew them, and by his skillful maneuvers decided the issue of the second day's fight.* The conquest of the duchy of Milan was the result of this victory, and peace supervening, the Duke of Alençon returned to France.

It was at this period that Margaret began to keep a Court, which, according to Odolant Desnos, rivaled that of her brother. We know that in 1517 she and her husband entertained the King with a series of magnificent fêtes at their Château of Alençon, which then combined both a palace and a fortress. But little of the château now remains, as, after the damage done to it during the religious wars between 1561 and 1572, it was partially demolished by Henry IV when he and Biron captured it in 1590. Still the lofty keep built by Henry I of England subsisted intact till in 1715 it was damaged by fire, and finally in 1787 razed to the ground.

The old pile was yet in all its splendor in 1517, when Francis I was entertained there with jousts and tournaments. At these gay gatherings Margaret appeared appareled in keeping with her brother's love of

---

* Odolant Desnos's *Mémoires historiques sur Alençon*, vol. ii. p. 238.

display; for, like all princesses, she clothed herself on important occasions in sumptuous garments. But in everyday life she was very simple, despising the vulgar plan of impressing the crowd by magnificence and splendor. In a portrait executed about this period, her dark-colored dress is surmounted by a wimple with a double collar and her head covered with a cap in the Bearnese style. This portrait* tends, like those of a later date, to the belief that Margaret's beauty, so celebrated by the poets of her time, consisted mainly in the nobility of her bearing and the sweetness and liveliness spread over her features. Her eyes, nose, and mouth were very large, but although she had been violently attacked with smallpox while still young, she had been spared the traces which this cruel illness so often left in those days, and she even preserved the freshness of her complexion until late in life.†

Like her brother, whom she greatly resembled, she was very tall. Her gait was solemn, but the dignified air of her person was tempered by extreme affability and a lively humor, which never left her.‡

Francis I did not allow the magnificent reception accorded to him at Alençon to pass unrewarded. He presented his sister with the duchy of Berry, where she henceforward exercised temporal control, though she does not appear to have ever resided there for any length of time. In 1521, when her husband started to the relief of Chevalier Bayard, attacked in Mézières by the Imperial troops, she repaired to Meaux with her mother so as to be near to the Duke. Whilst sojourning there she improved her acquaintance with the Bishop, William Briçonnet, who had gathered around him Gerard Roussel, Michael d'Arande, Lefèvre d'Etaples, and other celebrated disciples of the Reformation. The effect of Luther's preaching had scarcely reached France before Margaret had begun to manifest great interest in the movement, and had engaged in

---

* It is preserved at the Bibliothèque Nationale in Paris, where it will be found in the *Recueil de Portraits au crayon par Clouett Dumonstier, &c,* fol. xi.

† Referring to this subject, she says in one of her letters: "You can tell it to the Count and Countess of Vertus, whom you will go and visit on my behalf; and say to the Countess that I am sorely vexed that she has this loathsome illness. However, I had it as severely as ever was known. And if it be that she has caught it as I have been told, I should like to be near her to preserve her complexion, and do for her what I did for myself." — Génin's *lettres de Marguerite d'Angoulême,* Paris, 1841, p. 374.

‡ Sainte-Marthe says on this subject: "For in her face, in her gestures, in her walk, in her words, in all that she did and said, a royal gravity made itself so manifest and apparent, that one saw I know not what of majesty which compelled everyone to revere and dread her. In seeing her kindly receive everyone, refuse no one, and patiently listen to all, you would have promised yourself easy and facile access to her; but if she cast eyes upon you, there was in her face I know not what of gravity, which made you so astounded that you no longer had power, I do not say to walk a step, but even to stir a foot to approach her." — *Oraison-funèbre, &c,* p. 53.

a long correspondence with Briçonnet, which is still extant. Historians are at variance as to whether Margaret ever really contemplated a change of religion, or whether the protection she extended to the Reformers was simply dictated by a natural feeling of compassion and a horror of persecution. It has been contended that she really meditated a change of faith, and even attempted to convert her mother and brother; and this view is borne out by some passages in the letters which she wrote to Bishop Briçonnet after spending the winter of 1521 at Meaux.

Whilst she was sojourning there, her husband, having contributed to the relief of Mézières, joined the King, who was then encamped at Fervacques on the Somme, and preparing to invade Hainault. It was at this juncture that Clement Marot, the poet, who, after being attached to the person of Anne of Brittany, had become a hanger-on at the Court of Francis I, applied to Margaret to take him into her service.*

Shortly afterwards we find him furnishing her with information respecting the royal army, which had entered Hainault and was fighting there.†

Lenglet-Dufresnoy, in his edition of Marot's works, originated the theory that the numerous poems composed by Marot in honor of Margaret supply proofs of an amorous intrigue between the pair. Other authorities have endorsed this view; but M. Le Roux de Lincy asserts that in the pieces referred to, and others in which Marot incidentally speaks of Margaret, he can find no trace either of the fancy ascribed to her for the poet or of the passion which the latter may have felt for her. Like all those who surrounded the Duchess of Alençon, Marot, he remarks, exalted her beauty, art, and talent to the clouds; but whenever it is to her that his verses are directly addressed, he does not depart from the respect he owes to her. To give some likelihood to his conjectures, Lenglet-Dufresnoy had to suppose that Marot addressed Margaret in certain verses which were not intended for her. In the epistles previously mentioned, and in several short pieces, rondeaux, epigrams, new years' addresses, and epitaphs really written to or for the sister of Francis I, one only finds respectful praise, such as the humble courtier may fittingly offer to his patroness. There is nothing whatever, adds M. Le Roux de Lincy, to promote the suspicion that a passion, either unfortunate or favored, inspired a single one of these compositions.

The campaign in which Francis I was engaged at the time when Marot's connection with Margaret began, and concerning which the poet supplied her with information, was destined to influence the whole

---

* Epistle ii.: *Le Despourveu à Madame la Duchesse d'Alençon,* in the *Œuvres de Clément Marot,* 1700, vol. i. p. 99.

† Epistle iii.: *Du Camp d' Attigny à ma dite Dame d' Alençon, ibid.,* vol. i. p. 104.

reign, since it furnished the occasion of the first open quarrel between Francis I and the companion of his childhood, Charles de Bourbon, Count of Montpensier, and Constable of France. Yielding too readily on this occasion to the persuasions of his mother, Francis entrusted to Margaret's husband the command of the vanguard, a post which the Constable considered his own by virtue of his office. He felt mortally offended at the preference given to the Duke of Alençon, and from that day forward he and Francis were enemies forever.

Whilst the King was secretly jealous of Bourbon, who was one of the handsomest, richest, and bravest men in the kingdom, Louise of Savoy, although forty-four years of age, was in love with him. The Constable, then thirty-two, had lost his wife, Susan de Bourbon, from whom he had inherited vast possessions. To these Louise of Savoy, finding her passion disregarded, laid claim, as being a nearer relative of the deceased. A marriage, as Chancellor Duprat suggested, would have served to reconcile the parties, but the Constable having rejected the proposed alliance — with disdain, so it is said — the suit was brought before the Parliament and decided in favor of Louise. Such satisfaction as she may have felt was not, however, of long duration, for Charles de Bourbon left France, entered the service of Charles V, and in the following year (1524) helped to drive the French under Bonnivet out of Italy.

II

The Regency of Louise of Savoy — Margaret and the royal children — The defeat of Pavia and the death of the Duke of Alençon — The Royal Trinity — "All is lost save honor" — Margaret's journey to Spain and her negotiations with Charles V. — Her departure from Madrid — The scheme to arrest her, and her flight on horseback — Liberation of Francis I — Clever escape of Henry of Navarre from prison — Margaret's secret fancy for him — *Her personal appearance at this period* — *Marriage of Henry and Margaret at St. Germain.*

The most memorable events of Margaret's public life date from this period. Francis, who was determined to reconquer the Milanese, at once made preparations for a new campaign. Louise of Savoy was again appointed Regent of the kingdom, and as Francis's wife, Claude, was dying of consumption, the royal children were confided to the care of Margaret, whose husband accompanied the army. Louise of Savoy at first repaired to Lyons with her children, in order to be nearer to Italy, but she and Margaret soon returned to Blois, where the Queen was dying. Before the royal army had reached Milan Claude expired, and soon afterwards Louise was incapacitated by a violent attack of gout, while the children of Francis also fell ill. The little ones, of whom Margaret had charge, consisted of three boys and three girls, the former being Francis, the Dauphin, who died in 1536, Charles, Duke of Orleans, who died in 1545, and Henry, Count of Angoulême, who succeeded his father on the throne. The girls comprised Madeleine, afterwards the wife of James V of Scotland, Margaret, subsequently Duchess of Savoy, and the Princess Charlotte. The latter was particularly beloved by her aunt Margaret, who subsequently dedicated to her memory her poem *Le Miroir de l'Ame Pécheresse.* While the other children recovered from their illness, little Charlotte, as Margaret records in her letters to Bishop Briçonnet, was seized "with so grievous a malady of fever and flux," that after a month's suffering she expired, to the deep grief of her aunt, who throughout her illness had scarcely left her side.

This affliction was but the beginning of Margaret's troubles. Soon afterwards the Constable de Bourbon, in conjunction with Pescara and Lannoy, avenged his grievances under the walls of Pavia. On this occasion, as at Marignano, the Duke of Alençon commanded the French reserves, and had charge of the fortified camp from which Francis, listening to Bonnivet, sallied forth, despite the advice of his best officers. The King bore himself bravely, but he was badly wounded and forced to surrender, after La Palisse, Lescun, Bonnivet, La Trémoïlle, and Bussy d'Amboise had been slain before his eyes. Charles of Alençon was then unable to resist the advice given him to retreat, and thus save the few Frenchmen who had escaped the arms of the Imperialists. With four hundred lances he abandoned the camp, crossed the Ticino, and reaching France by way of Piedmont, proceeded to Lyons, where he found Louise of Savoy and Margaret.

It has been alleged that they received him with harsh reproaches, and that, unable to bear the shame he felt for his conduct, he died only a few days after the battle.*

There are several errors in these assertions, which a contemporary document enables us to rectify. The battle of Pavia was fought on February 14th, 1525, and Charles of Alençon did not die till April 11th, more than a month after his arrival at Lyons. He was carried off in five days by pleurisy, and some hours before his death was still able to rise and partake of the communion. Margaret bestowed the most tender care upon him, and the Regent herself came to visit him, the Duke finding strength enough to say to her, "Madam, I beg of you to let the King know that since the day he was made a prisoner I have been expecting nothing but death, since I was not sufficiently favored by Heaven to share his lot or to be slain in serving him who is my king, father, brother, and good master." After kissing the Regent's hand he added, "I commend to you her who has been my wife for fifteen years, and who has been as good as she is virtuous towards me." Then, as Louise of Savoy wished to take Margaret away, Charles turned towards the latter and said to her, "Do not leave me."

The Duchess refused to follow her mother, and embracing her dying husband, showed him the crucifix placed before his eyes. The Duke, having summoned one of his gentlemen, M. de Chandeniers, instructed him to bid farewell on his part to all his servants, and to thank them for their services, telling them that he had no longer strength to see them. He asked God aloud to forgive his sins, received the extreme unction from the Bishop of Lisieux, and raising his eyes to heaven, said "Jesus," and expired.†

Whilst tending her dying husband, Margaret was also deeply concerned as to the fate of her captive brother, for whom she always evinced the warmest affection. Indeed, so close were the ties uniting Louise of Savoy and her two children that they were habitually called the "Trinity," as Clement Marot and Margaret have recorded in their poems.‡

In this Trinity Francis occupied the highest place; his mother called him "her Cæsar and triumphant hero," while his sister absolutely

---

* See Garnier's *Histoire de France*, vol. xxiv.; Gaillard's *Histoire de France*, *&c.* Odolant Desnos, usually well informed, falls into the same error, and asserts that when the Duke, upon his arrival, asked Margaret to kiss him, she replied, "Fly, coward! you have feared death. You might find it in my arms, as I do not answer for myself." — *Mémoires historiques*, vol. ii. p. 253.

† From a MS. poem in the Bibliothèque Nationale entitled *Les Prisons*, probably written by William Philander or Filandrier, a canon of Rodez.

‡ See *Œuvres de Clément Marot*, 1731, vol. v. p. 274; and A. Champoîlion-Figeac's *Poésies de François Ier, &c.*, Paris, 1847, p. 80.

reverenced him, and was ever ready to do his bidding. Thus the intelligence that he was wounded and a prisoner threw them into consternation, and they were yet undecided how to act when they received that famous epistle in which Francis wrote — not the legendary words, "All is lost save honor," but — "Of all things there have remained to me but honor and life, which is safe." After begging his mother and sister to face the extremity by employing their customary prudence, the King commended his children to their care, and expressed the hope that God would not abandon him.* This missive revived the courage of the Regent and Margaret, for shortly afterwards we find the latter writing to Francis: "Your letter has had such effect upon the health of Madame [Louise], and of all those who love you, that it has been to us as a Holy Ghost after the agony of the Passion. . . . Madame has felt so great a renewal of strength, that whilst day and evening last not a moment is lost over your business, so that you need have no grief or care about your kingdom and children."†

Louise of Savoy was indeed now displaying courage and ability. News shortly arrived that the King had been transferred to Madrid, and that Charles demanded most onerous conditions for the release of his prisoner. At this juncture Francis wrote to his mother that he was very ill, and begged of her to come to him. Louise, however, felt that she ought not to accede to this request, for it would be jeopardizing the monarchy to place the Regent as well as the King of France in the Emperor's hands; accordingly she resolved that Margaret should go instead of herself.

The Baron of St. Blancard, general of the King's galleys, who had previously offered to rescue Francis while the latter was on his way to Spain, received orders to make the necessary preparations for Margaret's voyage, of which she defrayed the expense, as is shown by a letter she wrote to John Brinon, Chancellor of Alençon. In this missive she states that the Baron of St. Blancard has made numerous disbursements on account of her journey which are to be refunded to him, "so that he may know that I am not ungrateful for the good service he has done me, for he hath acquitted himself thereof in such a way that I have occasion to be gratified."‡

---

* See extract from the Registers of the Parliament of Paris (Nov. 10, 1525) in Dulaure's *Histoire de Paris,* Paris, 1837, vol. iii. p. 209; and Lalanne's *Journal d'un Bourgeois de Paris,* Paris, 1854, p. 234. The original of the letter no longer exists, but the authenticity of the text cannot be disputed, as all the more essential portions are quoted in the collective reply of Margaret and Louise of Savoy, which is still extant. See Champollion-Figeac's Captivité de François Ier, pp. 129, 130.

† Génin's *Nouvelles Lettres de la Peine de Navarre,* Paris, 1842, p. 27.

‡ Génin's *Lettres de Marguerite, &c,* p. 193. — Génin's Notice, *ibid.,* p. 19.

Despite adverse winds, Margaret embarked on August 27th, 1525, at Aigues-Mortes, with the President de Selves, the Archbishop of Embrun, the Bishop of Tarbes, and a fairly numerous suite of ladies. The Emperor had granted her a safe-conduct for six months, and upon landing in Spain she hurried to Madrid, where she found her brother very sick both in mind and body. She eagerly caressed and tended him, and with a good result, as she knew his nature and constitution much better than the doctors. To raise his depressed spirits she had recourse to religious ceremonies, giving orders for an altar to be erected in the room where he was lying. She then requested the Archbishop of Embrun to celebrate mass, and received the communion in company of all the French retainers about the prisoner. It is stated that the King, who for some hours had given no sign of life, opened his eyes at the moment of the consecration of the elements, and asked for the communion, saying, "God will cure me, soul and body." From this time forward he began to recover his health, though he remained fretful on account of his captivity.

It was a difficult task to obtain his release. The Court and the Emperor were extremely polite, but Margaret soon recognized the emptiness of their protestations of good-will. "They all tell me that they love the King," she wrote, "but I have little proof of it. If I had to do with honest folks, who understand what honor is, I should not care, but it is the contrary."*

She was not the woman to turn back at the first obstacle, however; she began by endeavoring to gain over several high personages, and on perceiving that the men avoided speaking with her on serious business, she addressed herself to their mothers, wives, or daughters. In a letter to Marshal de Montmorency, then with the King, she thus refers to the Duke del Infantado, who had received her at his castle of Guadalaxara. "You will tell the King that the Duke has been warned from the Court that if he wishes to please the Emperor neither he nor his son is to speak to me; but the ladies are not forbidden me, and to them I will speak twofold."†

Throughout the negotiations for her brother's release Margaret always maintained the dignity and reserve fitting to her sex and situation. Writing to Francis on this subject she says: "The Viceroy (Lannoy) has sent me word that he is of opinion I should go and see the Emperor, but I have told him through M. de Senlis that I have not yet stirred from my lodging without being asked, and that whenever it pleases the Emperor to see me I shall be found there."‡

---

* *Lettres de Marguerite, &c.,* p. 21.
† *Lettres de Marguerite, &c.,* p. 197.

Margaret was repeatedly admitted to the Imperial council to discuss the conditions of her brother's ransom. She showed as much ability as loftiness of mind on these occasions, and several times won Charles V himself and the sternest of his Ministers to her opinion.*

She highly favored the proposed marriage between Francis and his rival's sister, Eleanor of Austria, detecting in this alliance the most certain means of a speedy release. Eleanor, born at Louvain in 1498, had in 1519 married Emanuel, King of Portugal, who died two years afterwards. Since then she had been promised to the Constable de Bourbon, but the Emperor did not hesitate to sacrifice the latter to his own interests.

He himself, being fascinated by Margaret's grace and wit, thought of marrying her, and had a letter sent to Louise of Savoy, plainly setting forth the proposal. In this missive, referring to the Constable de Bourbon, Charles remarked that "there were good matches in France in plenty for him; for instance, Madame Renée,† with whom he might very well content himself."‡ These words have led to the belief that there had been some question of a marriage between Margaret and the Constable; however, there is no mention of any such alliance in the diplomatic documents exchanged between France and Spain on the subject of the King's release. These documents comprise an undertaking to restore the Constable his estates, and even to arrange a match for him in France,[1] but Margaret is never mentioned. She herself, in the numerous letters handed down to us, does not once refer to the famous exile,

---

[2] *Captivité de François Ier*, p. 358.

* Brantôme states that the Emperor was greatly impressed and astonished by her plain speaking. She reproached him for treating Francis so harshly, declaring that this course would not enable him to attain his ends. "For although he (the King) might die from the effects of this rigorous treatment, his death would not remain unpunished, as he had children who would some day become men and wreak signal vengeance." "These words," adds Brantôme, "spoken so bravely and in such hot anger, gave the Emperor occasion for thought, insomuch that he moderated himself and visited the King and made him many fine promises, which he did not keep, however." With the Ministers Margaret was even more outspoken; but we are told that she turned her oratorical powers "to such good purpose that she rendered herself agreeable rather than odious or unpleasant; the more readily as she was also good-looking, a widow, and in the flower of her age." — *Œuvres de Brantôme*, 8vo, vol. v. (*Les Dames illustres*).

† Renée, the younger daughter of Louis XII and Anne of Brittany, subsequently celebrated as Renée of Ferrara.

‡ This letter is preserved at the Bibliothèque Nationale, Béthune MSS., No. 8496, fol. xiii.

[1] *Captivité de Francois Ier, &c.*, pp. 167-207.

and the intrigue described by certain historians and romancers evidently rests upon no solid foundation.*

After three months of negotiations, continually broken off and renewed, Margaret and her brother, feeling convinced of Charles V's evil intentions, resolved to take steps to ensure the independence of France. By the King's orders Robertet, his secretary, drew up letters-patent, dated November 1525 by which it was decreed that the young Dauphin should be crowned at once, and that the regency should continue in the hands of Louise of Savoy, but that in the event of her death the same power should be exercised by Francis's "very dear and well-beloved only sister, Margaret of France, Duchess of Alençon and Berry."† However, all these provisions were to be deemed null and void in the event of Francis obtaining his release.

It has been erroneously alleged that Margaret on leaving Spain took this deed of abdication with her, and that the Emperor, informed of the circumstance, gave orders for her to be arrested as soon as her safe-conduct should expire.‡ However, it was the Marshal de Montmorency who carried the deed to France, and Charles V in ordering the arrest of Margaret had no other aim than that of securing an additional hostage in case his treaty with Francis should not be fulfilled.

Margaret, pressed by her brother, at last asked for authorization to leave Spain. By the manner in which the permission was granted she perceived that the Emperor wished to delay rather than hasten her journey. During November she wrote Francis a letter in which this conviction was plainly expressed, and about the 19th of the month she left Madrid upon her journey overland to France.

At first she traveled very leisurely, but eventually she received a message from her brother, advising her to hasten her speed, as the Emperor, hoping that she would still be in Spain in January, when her safe-conduct would expire, had given orders for her arrest. Accordingly, on reaching Medina-Celi she quitted her litter and mounted on horseback, accomplishing the remainder of her journey in the saddle. Nine or ten days before the safe-conduct expired she passed Perpignan and reached Salces, where some French nobles were awaiting her.

Soon after her return to France she again took charge of the royal children, who once more fell ill, this time with the measles, as Margaret

---

* Varillas is the principal historian who has mentioned this supposed intrigue, which also furnished the subject of a romance entitled *Histoire de Marguerite, Reine de Navarre, &c.,* 1696.

† *Captivité de François 1er, &c.,* p. 85.

‡ Génin's Notice in the *Lettres de Marguerite, &c.,* p. 25.

related in the following characteristic letter addressed to her brother, still a prisoner in Spain: —

"My Lord, — The fear that I have gone through about your children, without saying anything of it to Madame (Louise of Savoy), who was also very ill, obliges me to tell you in detail the pleasure I feel at their recovery. M. d'Angoulême caught the measles, with a long and severe fever; afterwards the Duke of Orleans took them with a little fever; and then Madame Madeleine without fever or pain; and by way of company the Dauphin without suffering or fever. And now they all are quite cured and very well; and the Dauphin does marvels in the way of studying, mingling with his schooling a hundred thousand other occupations. And there is no more question of passions, but rather of all the virtues; M. d'Orléans is nailed to his book, and says that he wants to be good; but M. d'Angoulême does more than the others, and says things that are to be esteemed rather as prophecies than childish utterances, which you, my lord, would be amazed to hear. Little Margot resembles myself; she will not be ill; but I am assured here that she has very graceful ways, and is getting prettier than ever Mademoiselle d'Angoulême* was."

Francis having consented to the onerous conditions imposed by Charles V, was at last liberated. On March 17th, 1526, he was exchanged for his two elder sons, who were to serve as hostages for his good faith, and set foot upon the territory of Beam. He owed Margaret a deep debt of gratitude for her efforts to hasten his release, and one of his first cares upon leaving Spain was to wed her again in a fitting manner. He appears to have opened matrimonial negotiations with Henry VIII of England,† but, fortunately for Margaret, without result. She, it seems, had already made her choice. There was then at the French Court a young King, without a kingdom, it is true, but endowed with numerous personal qualities. This was Henry d'Albret, Count of Beam, and legitimate sovereign of Navarre, then held by Charles V in defiance of treaty rights. Henry had been taken prisoner with Francis at Pavia and confined in the fortress there, from which, however, he had managed to escape in the following manner.

Having procured a rope ladder in view of descending from the castle, he ordered Francis de Rochefort, his page, to get into his bed and feign sleep. Then he descended by the rope, the Baron of Arros and a valet following him. In the morning, when the captain on duty came to see Henry, as was his usual custom, he was asked by a page to let the King sleep on, as he had been very ill during the night. Thus the trick was

---

* Génin's *Lettres de Marguerite, &c,* p. 70. The Mademoiselle d'Angoulême alluded to at the end of the letter is Margaret herself.

† *Lettres de Marguerite, &c,* p. 31.

only discovered when the greater part of the day had gone by, and the fugitives were already beyond pursuit.*

As the young King of Navarre had spent a part of his youth at the French Court, he was well known to Margaret, who apparently had a secret fancy for him. He was in his twenty-fourth year, prepossessing, and extremely brave.† There was certainly a great disproportion of age between him and Margaret, but this must have served to increase rather than attenuate her passion. She herself was already thirty-five, and judging by a portrait executed about this period,‡ in which she is represented in mourning for the Duke of Alençon, with a long veil falling from her cap, her personal appearance was scarcely prepossessing.

The proposed alliance met with the approval of Francis, who behaved generously to his sister. He granted her for life the enjoyment of the duchies of Alençon and Berry, with the counties of Armagnac and Le Perche and several other lordships. Finally, the marriage was celebrated on January 24th, 1527, at St. Germain-en-Laye, where, as Sauvai records, "there were jousts, tourneying, and great triumph for the space of eight days or thereabouts."[1]

III

The retirement of King Henry to Beam — Margaret's intercourse with her brother — The inscription at Chambord — Margaret's adventure with Bonnivet — Margaret's relations with her husband — Her opinions upon love and conjugal fidelity — Her confinements and her children — The Court in Beam and the refugee Reformers — Margaret's first poems — Her devices, pastorals, and mysteries — The embellishment of Pau —

---

* Olhagaray's *Histoire de Faix, Beam, Navarre, &c,* Paris, 1609. p. 487.
† He was born at Sanguesa, April 1503, and became King of Navarre in 1517.
‡ This portrait is at the Bibliothèque Nationale in the *Recueil de Portraits au crayon* by Clouet, Dumonstier, &c. (fol. 88).
[1] *Antiquités de Paris,* vol. ii. p. 688.

Margaret at table and in her study — Reforms and improvements in Beam — Works of defense at Navarreinx — Scheme of refortifying Sauveterre.

Some historians have stated that in wedding his sister to Henry d'Albret, Francis pledged himself to compel Charles V to surrender his brother-in-law's kingdom of Navarre. This, however, was but a political project, of which no deed guaranteed the execution. Francis no doubt promised Margaret to make every effort to further the restitution, and she constantly reminded him of his promise, as is shown by several of her letters. However, political exigencies prevented Francis from carrying out his plans, and in a diplomatic document concerning the release of the children whom Charles held as hostages the following clause occurs: "Item, the said Lord King promises not to help or favor the King of Navarre (although he has married his only and dear beloved sister) in reconquering his kingdom."[*]

The indifference shown by Francis for the political fortunes of his brother-in-law, despite the numerous and signal services the latter had rendered him, justly discontented Henry, who at last resolved to withdraw from the Court, where Montmorency, Brion, and several other personages, his declared enemies, were in favor. Margaret apparently had to follow her husband in his retirement, for Sainte-Marthe remarks: "When the King of Navarre, disgusted with the Court, and seeing none of the promises that his brother-in-law had made him realized, resolved to withdraw to Beam, Margaret, although the keen air of the mountains was hurtful to her health, and her doctors had threatened her with a premature death if she persevered in braving the rigors of the climate, preferred to put her life in peril rather than to fail in her duty by not accompanying her husband."[†]

Various biographers express the opinion that this retirement took place in 1529, shortly after the Peace of Cambray, and others give 1530 as the probable date. Margaret, we find, paid a flying visit to Beam with her husband in 1527; on January 7th, 1528, she was confined of her first child, Jane, at Fontainebleau, and the following year she is found with her little daughter at Longray, near Alençon. In 1530 she is confined at Blois of a second child, John, Prince of Viana, who died at Alençon on Christmas Day in the same year, when but five and a half months old. Then in 1531 her letters show her with her mother at Fontainebleau; and Louise of Savoy being stricken with the plague, then raging in

---

[*] Bibliothèque Nationale, MS. No. 8546 (Béthune), fol. 107.
[†] *Oraison funèbre,* &c, p. 70.

France, Margaret closes her eyes at Gretz, a little village between Fontainebleau and Nemours, on September 22nd in that year.

It was after this event that the King and Queen of Navarre determined to proceed to Beam, but so far as Margaret herself is concerned, it is certain that retirement was never of long duration whilst her brother lived. She is constantly to be found at Alençon, Fontainebleau, and Paris, being frequently with the King, who did not like to remain separated from her for any length of time. He was wont to initiate her into his political intrigues in view of availing himself of her keen and subtle mind. Brantôme, referring to this subject, remarks that her wisdom was such that the ambassadors who "spoke to her were greatly charmed by it, and made great report of it to those of their nation on their return; in this respect she relieved the King her brother, for they (the ambassadors) always sought her after delivering the chief business of their embassy, and often when there was important business the King handed it over to her, relying upon her for its definite resolution. She understood very well how to entertain and satisfy the ambassadors with fine speeches, of which she was very lavish, and also very clever at worming their secrets out of them, for which reason the King often said that she helped him right well and relieved him of a great deal."*

Margaret's own letters supply proof of this. She is constantly to be found intervening in state affairs and exercising her influence. She receives the deputies from Basle, Berne, and Strasburg who came to Paris in 1537 to ask Francis I for the release of the imprisoned Protestants. She joins the King at Valence when he is making preparations for a fresh war against Charles V; then she visits Montmorency at the camp of Avignon, which she praises to her brother; next, hastening to Picardy, when the Flemish troops are invading it, she writes from Amiens and speaks of Thérouenne and Boulogne, which she has found well fortified.

Francis, however, did not value her society and counsel solely for political reasons; he was also fond of conversing with her on literature, and at times they composed amatory verses together. According to an oft-repeated tradition, one day at the Château of Chambord, whilst Margaret was boasting to her brother of the superiority of womankind in matters of love, the King took a diamond ring from his finger and wrote on one of the windowpanes this couplet: —

"Souvent femme varie, Bien fol est qui s'y fie."†

---

* *Œuvres de Brantôme*, 8vo, vol. v. p. 222.
† "Woman is often fickle,
    Crazy indeed is he who trusts her."

Brantôme, who declares that he saw the inscription, adds, however, that it consisted merely of three words, "Toute femme varie" (all women are fickle), inscribed in *large* letters at the side of the window.* He says nothing of any pane of glass (all windowpanes were then extremely *small)* or of a diamond having been used;† and in all probability Francis simply traced these words with a piece of chalk or charcoal on the side of one of the deep embrasures, which are still to be seen in the windows of the château.

Margaret carried her complaisance for her brother so far as to excuse his illicit amours, and she was usually on the best of terms with his favorites.‡ It has been asserted that improper relations existed between the brother and sister, but this charge rests solely upon an undated letter from her to Francis, which may be interpreted in a variety of ways. Count de la Ferrière, in his introduction to Margaret's record of her expenditure,[1] expresses the opinion that it was penned in 1525, prior to her hasty departure from Spain; while M. Le Roux de Lincy assigns it to a later date, remarking that it was probably written during one of the frequent quarrels which arose between Margaret's brother and her husband. However, they are both of opinion that the letter does not bear the interpretation which other writers have placed upon it.[2]

The only really well-authenticated love intrigue in which Margaret was concerned — and in that she played a remarkably virtuous part — was her adventure with the Admiral de Bonnivet, upon which the fourth story of the *Heptameron* is based.[3] She was certainly unfortunate in both her marriages. Her life with the Duke of Alençon has already been spoken of; and as regards her second union, although contracted under apparently favorable auspices, it failed to yield Margaret the happiness she had hoped for. But four years after its celebration she wrote to the Marshal de Montmorency: "Since you are with the King of Navarre, I have no fear but that all will go well, provided you can keep him from falling in love with the Spanish ladies."** And again: "My nephew, I have received the letters you wrote to me, by which I have learnt that you are a much better relation than the King of Navarre is a good

---

* *Vies des Dames galantes,* Disc. iv.

† The practice of cutting glass with diamonds does not seem to have been resorted to until the close of the sixteenth century. See *Les Subtiles et Plaisantes Inventions de J. Prévost,* Lyons, 1584, part i. pp. 30, 31.

‡ E. Fournier's *L'Esprit dans l'Histoire,* Paris, 1860, p. 132 *et seq.*

[1] *Livre de Dépenses de Marguerite d'Angoulême, &c.* (Introduction).

[2] See *Lettres de Marguerite, &c.,* p. 246.

[3] Particulars concerning this adventure will be found in the notes to Tale iv., and also in the Appendix to the present volume (C).

** *Lettres de Marguerite, &c.,* p. 246.

husband, for you alone have given me news of the King (Francis) and of him, without his being willing to give pleasure to a poor wife, big with child, by writing a single word to her."[*]

In another letter written to the Marshal at the same period she says: "If you listen to the King of Navarre, he will make you commit so many disorders that he will ruin you."[†] Perhaps these words should not be taken literally; still they furnish cause for reflection when it is remembered that they were written by a woman just turned forty concerning her husband who was not yet thirty years old.

Margaret's views upon love and the affinity of souls were somewhat singular, but they indicate an elevated and generous nature. In several passages of the *Heptameron* she has expressed her opinion on these matters, ardently defending the honor of her sex and condemning those wives who show themselves indulgent as regards their husbands' infidelities.[‡] She blames those who sow dissension between husbands and wives, leading them on to blows;[1] and when someone asked her what she understood perfect love to be, she made answer, "I call perfect lovers those who seek some perfection in the object of their love, be it beauty, kindness, or good grace, tending to virtue, and who have such high and honest hearts that they will not even for fear of death do base things that honor and conscience blame."

In reference to this subject of conjugal fidelity a curious story is told of Margaret. One day at Mont-de-Marsan, upon seeing a young man convicted of having murdered his father being led to execution, she remarked to those about her that it was very wrong to put to death a young fellow who had not committed the crime imputed to him. It was pointed out to her that the judges had only condemned him upon conclusive proofs and the acknowledgments that he himself had made. Margaret, however, persisted in her remark, whereupon some of her intimates begged of her to justify it, for it seemed to them at least singular. "I do not doubt," she replied, "that this poor wretch killed his mother's husband, but he certainly did not kill his own father."[2]

Besides being unfortunate as regards her husbands, Margaret was also denied a mother's privileges. She experienced great suffering at her confinements,[3] and on two occasions she was delivered of still-born infants of the female sex.

---

[*]   *Ibid.*, p. 248.

[†]   *Lettres de Marguerite, &c,* p. 251.

[‡]   Epilogue of Tale xxxvii.

[1]   Epilogue of Tale xlvi.

[2]   Gabriel de Minut's *De la Beauté, Discours divers, &c.,* Lyons, 1587. p. 74.

[3]   *Nouvelles Lettres de Marguerite,* pp. 84 and 93.

She had centered many hopes upon her little boy, John, of whom she was confined without accident, but he died, as already stated, in infancy, and this misfortune was a great shock to her, though she tried to conceal it by having the Te Deum sung at the funeral in lieu of the ordinary service, and by setting up in the streets of Alençon the inscription, "God gave him, God has taken him away." However, from that time forward she never laid aside her black dress, though later on she wore it trimmed with marten's fur. Her best known portrait* represents her attired in this style with the quaint Bearnese cap, which she had also adopted, set upon her head.

Not only did Margaret lose her son by death, but she was prevented from enjoying the companionship of her daughter Jane. Francis, who never once lost sight of his own interests, deemed it advisable to possess himself of this child, who was the heiress to the throne of Navarre. Accordingly when Jane was but two years old she was sent by the King to the Château of Plessis-lès-Tours, where she was carefully brought up in strict seclusion.

To the fact that Margaret was never really happy with either of her husbands, and that she was precluded from discharging a mother's duties, one may ascribe, in part, her fondness for gathering round her a Court in which divines, scholars, and wits prominently figured. The great interest which she took in religious matters, as is shown by so many of her letters,† led her to shelter many of the persecuted Reformers in Beam; others she saved from the stake, and frequently in writing to the King and Marshal de Montmorency she begs for the release of some imprisoned heretic.

Margaret's religious views frequently caused dissension between her and her husband, in whose presence she abstained from giving expression to them. Hilarion de Coste mentions that "King Henry having one day been informed that a form of prayer and instruction contrary to

---

* Bibliothèque Nationale, *Recueil de Portraits au crayon, &c.,* fol. 46.

† One of these letters, written by her either to Philiberta of Savoy, Duchess of Nemours, or to Charlotte d'Orléans, Duchess of Nemours, both of whom were her aunts, may be thus rendered in English: "My aunt, on leaving Paris to escort the King, Monsieur de Meaux (Bishop Briçonnet), sent me the Gospels in French, translated by Fabry, word for word, which he says we should read with as much reverence and as much preparation to receive the Spirit of God, such as He has left it us in His Holy Scriptures, as when we go to receive it in the form of Sacrament. And inasmuch as Monsieur de Villeroy has promised to deliver them to you, I have requested him to do so, for these words (the Gospels) must not fall into evil hands. I beg, my aunt, that if by their means God grants you some grace, you will not forget her who is above all else your good niece and sister, Margaret." Fabry's translation of the Gospels was made in 1523-24.

that of his fathers was held in the chamber of the Queen, his wife, entered it intending to chastise the minister, and finding that he had been hurried away, the remains of his anger fell upon his wife, who received a blow from him, he remarking, 'Madam, you want to know too much about it,' and he at once sent word of the matter to King Francis."

It was at Nérac that most of the divines protected by Margaret found a refuge from the persecutions of the Sorbonne. Here she kept court in a castle of which there now only remains a vaulted fifteenth-century gallery formerly belonging to the northern wing. Nérac has, however, retained intact a couple of quaint mediaeval bridges, which Margaret must have ofttimes crossed in her many journeyings. Moreover, the townsfolk still point out the so-called Palace of Marianne, said to have been built by Margaret's husband for one of his mistresses, and also the old royal baths, which the Queen no doubt frequented.

It was at the castle of Nérac that Margaret's favorite protégé, the venerable Lefèvre d'Étaples, died at the age of one hundred and one, in the presence of his patroness, to whom before expiring he declared that he had never known a woman carnally in his life. However, he regretfully added that in his estimation he had been guilty of a greater sin, for he had neglected to lay down his life for his faith. Another partisan of the Reform, Gerard Roussel, whom Margaret had almost snatched from the stake and appointed Bishop of Oloron, had no occasion to express any such regret. His own flock speedily espoused the doctrines of the Reformation, but when he proceeded to Mauléon and tried to preach there, the Basques refused to listen to him, and hacked the pulpit to pieces, the Bishop being precipitated upon the flagstones, and so grievously injured that he died.

Beside the divines who sought an asylum at Nérac, there were various noted men of letters, foremost among whom we may class the Queen's two secretaries, Clement Marot, the poet, and Peter Le Maçon, the translator of Boccaccio's *Decameron*. This translation was undertaken at the Queen's request, as Le Maçon states in his dedication to her, and it has always been considered one of the most able literary works of the period. With Marot and Le Maçon, but in the more humble capacity of valet, at the yearly wages of one hundred and ten livres, there came the gay Bonaventure Despériers, the author of *Les Joyeux Devis*;* other writers, such as John Frotté, John de la Haye and Gabriel Chapuis, were also among Margaret's retainers.

---

* *Livre de Dépenses de Marguerite d'Angoulême.*

She herself had long practiced the writing of verses. It was in 1531, and at Alençon, that she issued her first volume of poems, the *Miroir de l'Ame Pécheresse,** which created a great stir at the time, for when it was re-issued in Paris by Augereau in 1533† the Sorbonne denounced it as unorthodox, and Margaret would have been branded as a heretic if Francis had not intervened and ordered the Rector of the Sorbonne to withdraw the decree censuring his sister's work. Nor did that content the King, for he caused Noël Béda, the syndic of the Faculty of Theology, to be arrested and confined in a dungeon at Mont St. Michel, where he perished miserably.

Margaret thus gained the day, but the annoyance she had been subjected to doubtless taught her to be prudent, for although she steadily went on writing, sixteen years elapsed before anymore of her poems were published. In the meantime various manuscript copies, some of which are still in existence, were made of them, notably one of the poem called "Débat d'Amour" by Margaret, and re-christened "La Coche" by her secretary, John de la Haye, when he subsequently published it in the *Marguerites de la Marguerite.* This manuscript is enriched with eleven curious miniatures, the last of which represents the Queen handing the volume bound in white velvet‡ to the Duchess of Etampes, her brother's mistress, whose qualities the poem extols. The Queen of Navarre was on the best of terms with this favorite, to whom in one of her letters she recommends certain servants.

Margaret was not only given to versifying, but was fond of framing devices, which she inscribed upon her books and furniture. At one time she adopted as her device a marigold turning towards the sun's rays, with the motto, "Non inferiora secutus," implying that she turned "all her acts, thoughts, will, and affections towards the great Sun of Justice, God Almighty."[1]

In her *Miroir de l'Ame Pécheresse,* previously referred to, there figures another device composed merely of the three words "Ung pour tout;" and in the manuscript of "La Coche" presented to the Duchess of Etampes, the motto "Plus vous que moys" is inscribed beneath each of the miniatures. Margaret also composed a series of devices for some jewels which her brother presented to his favorite, Madame de

---

* Brunet's *Manual,* 4th ed., vol. iii. p. 275.

† A second edition also appeared at Alençon in the same year.

‡ From the Queen's *Livre de Dépenses,* published by M. de la Ferrière, we learn that this MS., with the miniatures and binding, cost Margaret fifty golden crowns. It was formerly in the possession of M. Jérôme Pichon, and was afterwards acquired by M. Didot, at the sale of whose library it realized £804. The MS. was recently in the possession of M. de La Roche-la-Carelle.

[1] Claude Paradin's *Dévises héroïques,* Lyons, 1557, p. 41.

Châteaubriant. Respecting these Brantôme tells the following curious anecdote: —

"I have heard say, and hold on good authority, that when King Francis I had left Madame de Châteaubriant, his favorite mistress, to take Madame d'Etampes, as one nail drives out another, Madame d'Etampes begged the King to take back from the said Madame de Châteaubriant all the finest jewels that he had given her, not on account of their cost and value, for pearls and precious stones were not then so fashionable as they have been since, but for the love of the fine devices that were engraved and impressed upon them; which devices the Queen of Navarre, his sister, had made and composed, for she was a mistress in such matters.

"King Francis granted the request, and promised that he would do it. Having with this intent sent a gentleman to Madame de Châteaubriant to ask for the jewels, she at once feigned illness, and put the gentleman off for three days, when he was to have what he asked for. However, out of spite, she sent for a goldsmith, and made him melt down all these jewels without exception, and without having any respect for the handsome devices engraved upon them. And afterwards, when the said gentleman returned, she gave him all the jewels converted into gold ingots.

"'Go,' said she, 'and take these to the King, and tell him that since he has been pleased to take back from me that which he had given me so freely, I restore it and send it back in golden ingots. As for the devices, I have impressed them so firmly on my mind and hold them so dear in it, that I could not let anyone have and enjoy them save myself.'

"When the King had received all this, the ingots and the lady's remark, he only said, 'Take her back all. What I did was not for the value, for I would have restored her that twofold, but for the love of the devices, and since she has thus destroyed them, I do not want the gold, and send it back. She has shown in this matter more courage and generosity than it would have been thought could come from a woman.'"*

Besides writing verses and framing devices, Margaret, as Brantôme tells us, "often composed comedies and moralities, which were in those days styled pastorals, and which she had played by the young ladies of her Court."†

Hilarion de Coste states, moreover, that "she composed a tragicomic translation of almost the whole of the New Testament, which she caused to be played before the King, her husband, having assembled with this

---

* *Œuvres de Brantôme*, 8vo, vol. vii. p. 567.

† *Ibid.*, 8vo, vol. v. p. 219.

object some of the best actors of Italy; and as these buffoons are only born to give pleasure and make time pass away, in order to amuse the company they invariably introduced *rondeaux* and *virelais* against the ecclesiastics, especially the monks and village priests."*

These performances took place at the Château of Pau, which Margaret and her husband seem to have preferred to that of Nérac, though political reasons often compelled them to fix their abode at the latter. Pau, however, possessed the advantage of a mild climate, necessary for Margaret's health, besides being delightfully situated on the Bearnese Gave, the view from the château extending over a fertile valley limited by the snow-capped Pyrenees. There had been a château at Pau as early as the tenth century, but the oldest portions of the structure now subsisting date from the time of Edward III, when Pau was the capital of the celebrated Gaston-Phoebus. The château was considerably enlarged and embellished in the fifteenth century, but it was not until after Margaret's marriage with Henry d'Albret that the more remarkable decorative work was executed. Upon leaving Nérac to reside at Pau, Margaret summoned a number of Italian artists and confided the embellishment of the château to them.†

It was not, however, merely the château which Margaret beautified at Pau. Already at Alençon she had laid out a charming park, which a contemporary poet called a terrestrial paradise,‡ and upon coming to reside at Pau she transformed the surrounding woods into delightful gardens, pronounced to be the finest then existing in Europe.[1]

---

* M. Le Roux de Lincy points out that this statement is exaggerated, for Margaret, instead of turning the whole of the New Testament into verse, merely wrote four Mysteries which mainly dealt with the childhood of Christ.

† Some of the doors and windows of the château are elaborately ornamented in the best style of the Renaissance, whilst the grand staircase, although dating from Margaret's time, has vaulted arches, sometimes in the Romanesque and at others in the Gothic style. Entwined on the friezes are the initials H and M (Henry and Margaret), occasionally accompanied by the letter R, implying *Rex* or *Regina.* On the first floor of the château is the bedroom occupied by Margaret's husband, remarkable for its Renaissance chimneypiece, and also a grand reception hall, now adorned with tapestry made for Francis I in Flanders. It was in this latter room that the Count of Montgomery — the same who had thrust out the eye of Henry II at a tournament, and thereby caused that monarch's death — acting at the instigation of Margaret's daughter Jane, assembled the Catholic noblemen of Beam on August 24, 1569, and, after entertaining them with a banquet, had them treacherously massacred. Bascle de Lagrèze's *Château de Pau,* Paris, 1854.

‡ *Le Recueil de l'Antique pré-excellence de Gaule, &c.,* by G. Le Roville, Paris, 1551 (fol. 74).

[1] Hilarion de Coste's *Vies et Éloges des Dames illustres, &c.,* vol. ii. p. 272.

Some idea of their appearance may be gained from a couple of the miniatures adorning a curious manuscript catechism composed for Margaret and now in the Arsenal Library at Paris.*

The Court which Margaret kept in turns at Alençon, Nérac, and Pau does not appear to have been so sumptuous and gay as some of her biographers assert. Brantôme mentions that the Queen's two tables were always served with frugality, and Sainte-Marthe states that "she talked at dinner and supper now of medicine, of food wholesome or unwholesome for the human body, and of objects of nature with Masters Schyron, Cormier, and Esterpin, her expert and learned doctors, who carefully watched her eat and drink, as is done with princes; now she would speak of history or of the precepts of philosophy with other very erudite personages, with whom her house was never unfurnished; at another time she would enter into conversation on her faith and the Christian religion with Monsieur Gerard, Bishop of Oloron. Altogether there was not a single moment that was not employed by her in honest, pleasant, and useful conversation."†

The same panegyrist tells us of Margaret's favorite occupations, mentioning that when she was alone in her room she more often held a book in her hand than a distaff, a pen than a spindle, and the ivory of her tablets than a needle. He then adds: "And if she applied herself to tapestry or other needlework, such as was to her a pleasant occupation, she had beside her someone who read to her, either from a historian or a poet, or some other notable and useful author; or else she dictated some meditation which was written down."‡

Margaret's time was far from being wholly occupied in this manner, for she actively assisted her husband in carrying out improvements and

---

* *Manuscrits théologiques français*, No. 60, *Initiatoire Instruction en la Religion chrétienne, &c.* In one of these miniatures the Savior is represented carrying the cross, followed by Henry of Navarre, his brother Charles d'Albret, Margaret, and other personages, all of whom bear crosses, whilst in the background are some pleasure-grounds with a castle, a little waterfall, and a lake. Another miniature in the same manuscript shows King Henry of Navarre with a flower in his hand, which he seems to be offering to the Queen, who stands in the background among a party of courtiers. The King wears a surtout of cloth of gold, edged with ermine, over a blue jerkin, and a red cap with a white feather. Margaret is also arrayed in cloth of gold, but with a black cap and wimple. She is standing in a garden enclosed by a railing, and adorned with a fountain in the form of a temple which rises among groves and arbors. Beyond a white crenellated wall is a castle which has been identified with that of Pau. On fol. 1 of the same MS. the artist has depicted Queen Margaret's escutcheon, by which we find that she quartered the arms of France with those of Navarre, Aragon, Castile, Leon, Beam, Bigorre, Evreux, and Albret.

† *Oraison funèbre, &c*, p. 60.

‡ *Ibid.*, p. 68.

reforms in Beam. The result was that the country, naturally good and fertile, but left in bad condition, uncultivated and sterile through the carelessness of its inhabitants, soon changed its appearance owing to the efforts of Henry and his wife. From all the provinces of France laborers were attracted who settled there and improved and fertilized the fields.*

Henry d'Albret also devoted himself to the placing of the country in a proper state of defense, and fortified several of the towns. Navarreinx, commanding the valley of the Gave of Oloron, was virtually rebuilt by him and transformed into a perfect stronghold, as was evidenced during the religious wars, when it successfully withstood the artillery of Terrade, the Catholic commander. Long afterwards, when Vauban inaugurated his new system of fortification, he came to Navarreinx, and on seeing the ramparts raised by Margaret's husband was so favorably impressed, that instead of leveling them to the ground he contented himself with adding to them and making various improvements. Henry d'Albret was also anxious to refortify Sauveterre, which the Prince of Orange, with one of the Imperial armies, had captured in 1523, when he half-demolished the old castle of Montreal, then the most formidable citadel in Beam. However, as time and money were lacking, Henry had to abandon his plans, and the ruins left by the Imperialists, the ivy-clad keep, and mutilated bridge over the Gave soon fell into irremediable decay.†

IV

Margaret's attachment to her daughter — Refusal of Jane to marry the Duke of Clevés — Intervention of Margaret — The wedding at Châtelherault and the fall of the Constable de Montmorency — Margaret and her husband at Caulerets — The "Heptameron" — Illness and death of Francis I — Margaret's anxiety and grief — Her "Marguerites de la

---

* *Vies el Éloges des Dames illustres,* vol. ii. p. 272.
† M. Paul Perret's *Pyrénées françaises,* vol. ii. p. 303.

Marguerite" — Jane d'Albret's second marriage — Death of Margaret at Odos or Audaux — Her funeral at Lescar — Destruction of her tomb.

*W*hilst Margaret was living amongst divines and scholars at Pau and Nérac, her mind, as her letters indicate, constantly turned to her daughter Jane, whom Aimée de la Fayette, wife of the Bailiff of Caen, was bringing up at Plessis-lès-Tours. Margaret was only able to see Jane at rare intervals during some of her trips to France, and she was mainly indebted to sympathizing friends for news of the little Princess's condition and health. All her maternal tenderness was concentrated on this daughter, and whenever the child was ailing she became distracted.

Sainte-Marthe records that in December 1537, while Margaret was sojourning in Paris, her daughter, then scarcely nine years old, fell seriously ill at the royal house of Plessis-lès-Tours; and as it was rumored amongst the Court, then at Paris, that the Princess was threatened with death, her virtuous mother, Margaret, at about four o'clock in the evening, ordered her litter to be brought, saying that she would go and see her daughter, and that all her people should prepare to start. There was nothing ready, the officials and servants were absent, and scattered about the town of Paris and the neighboring villages. It was already dark, for this was during the shortest days of the year, the weather too was adverse on account of the rain, and neither her litter nor her baggage mules were at hand. Seeing this, the courageous Queen borrowed the litter of Madame Margaret, her niece,* got in it, and contenting herself with scant escort, started from Paris and went as far as Bourg-la-Reine.

"When they had arrived there she did not alight at her lodgings, but went straight to the church, which she at once entered, saying to those about her, that her heart told her I know not what concerning her daughter's fate, and affectionately begging them all to withdraw and leave her alone for an hour in the church. All obeyed and in great uneasiness waited for their mistress at the church door; the Sénéchale de Poitou,† a very faithful lady, and very solicitous about Margaret, alone entering with her. Margaret having gone in, kneels down before the image of Jesus crucified, prays to God from the depths of her heart, sighs, weeps, confesses all her transgressions, and laying to herself alone the cause of her daughter's illness, humbly asks pardon, and begs that the sufferer's restoration to health may be granted. After this act of faith Margaret felt relieved, and she had scarcely arrived at her lodgings when

---

* The daughter of Francis I, subsequently Duchess of Savoy.
† Brantôme's grandmother.

the Bishop of Mende came to announce to her that her daughter was in the way of recovery."*

When Jane was barely twelve years old Charles V asked her in marriage for his son Philip, but Francis, who was by no means anxious to see the Spaniards established on the northern side of the Pyrenees, preferred that the girl should marry William III, Duke of Cleves. It has frequently been asserted that Francis on this occasion exercised compulsion not only upon his niece, but also upon the King and Queen of Navarre, who vainly protested against this abuse of power. The truth is, that Margaret not only favored the marriage, but threatened to have Jane whipped if she persisted in her refusal. Moreover, the little bride having declared to Francis I that she protested against the alliance, Margaret wrote to her brother as follows: —

"My Lord, in my extreme desolation, I have only one single comfort, it is that of knowing with certainty that neither the King of Navarre nor myself have ever had any other wish or intention than that of obeying you, not only as regards a marriage, but in whatever you might order. But now, my lord, having heard that my daughter, neither recognizing the great honor you do her in deigning to visit her, nor the obedience that she owes you, nor that a girl should have no will of her own, has spoken to you so madly as to say to you that she begged of you she might not be married to M. de Cleves, I do not know, my lord, either what I ought to think of it, or what I ought to say to you about it, for I am grieved to the heart, and have neither relative nor friend in the world from whom I can seek advice or consolation. And the King of Navarre is on his part so amazed and grieved at it that I have never seen him before so provoked. I cannot imagine whence comes this great boldness, of which she had never spoken to us. She excuses herself towards us in that she is more intimate with you than with ourselves, but this intimacy should not give rise to such boldness, without ever as I know seeking advice from anyone, for if I knew any creature who had put such an idea into her head, I would make such a demonstration that you, my lord, would know that this madness is contrary to the will of the father and mother, who have never had, and never will have, any other than your own."†

The rebellion of Jane did not prevent the marriage, which was solemnized at Châtelherault on July 15th, 1540. According to some authorities, Francis was so determined upon the alliance that he required the Duke of Cleves to enter his bride's bed in the presence of witnesses, so that the marriage should be deemed beyond annulment.‡

---

* Oraison funèbre, &c, p. 38.
† *Nouvelles Lettres, &c.,* p. 176.

It was at Châtelherault on this occasion that Margaret triumphed over the Constable de Montmorency, who in earlier years had been her close friend, and with whom she had carried on such a voluminous correspondence. Montmorency had requited her good services with ingratitude, repeatedly endeavoring to estrange Francis from her. Brantôme gives an instance of this in the following passage: — "I have heard related," he says, "by a person of good faith that the Constable de Montmorency, then in the highest favor, speaking of this matter of religion one day with the King, made no difficulty or scruple about telling him, that 'if he really wished to exterminate the heretics of his kingdom, he ought to begin at his Court and with his nearest relatives, mentioning the Queen his sister,' to which the King replied, 'Do not speak of her; she loves me too much. She will never believe anything save what I believe, and will never take up a religion prejudicial to the State.'"*

As soon as Margaret became aware of Montmorency's conduct she ceased all correspondence with him and steadily endeavored to effect his overthrow, which was brought about on the occasion of Jane's marriage. "It was necessary to carry the little bride to the church," says Brantôme, "as she was laden with jewels and a dress of gold and silver, and owing to this and the weakness of her body, was not able to walk. So the King ordered the Constable to take his little niece and carry her to the church, at which all the Court were greatly astonished, for at such a ceremony this was a duty little suited and honorable for a Constable, and might very well have been given to another. However, the Queen of Navarre was in no way displeased, but said, 'Behold! he who wished to ruin me with the King my brother now serves to carry my daughter to church.' The Constable," adds Brantôme, "was greatly displeased at the task, and sorely vexed to serve as such a spectacle to everyone; and he began to say, 'It is now all over with my favor. Farewell to it.' Thus it happened, for after the wedding festival and dinner he had his dismissal and left at once."†

After the marriage of her daughter Margaret returned to Paris, and thence repaired to Mont-de-Marsan to spend the winter of 1540–41. Late in the following spring she went to Cauterets in the Pyrenees to take the baths. Writing during Lent to her brother she states that her husband

---

†† Henri Martin's *Histoire de France.* The marriage, however, was not really consummated (*Nouvelles Lettres, &c.,* pp. 236, 237), and it was eventually annulled by Pope Paul III, to whom Francis applied for a divorce when the Duke of Cleves deserted his cause for that of Charles V.

* *Œuvres de Brantôme,* 8vo, vol. v. (*Dames illustres*), p. 219.

† *Œuvres de Brantôme,* 8vo, vol. v. (*Dames illustres*), p. 220.

having had a fall will repair to Cauterets by the advice of his doctors,* and that she intends to accompany him to prevent him from worrying and to transact his business for him, "for when one is at the baths one must live like a child without any care."†

This was not her only motive in going to Cauterets apparently, for in a letter to Duke William of Cleves, her daughter's husband, dated April 1541, she states that as she is suffering from a *caterre* which "has fallen upon half her neck," and compels her to keep her bed, the doctors have advised her to take "the natural baths," and hope that she will be cured by the end of May, providing she follows all their prescriptions.‡

That this visit to Cauterets left a deep impression upon the mind of Margaret is evidenced by the work upon which her literary fame rests. The scene selected for the prologue of the *Heptameron* is Cauterets and the surrounding country; still it is evident that the book was not commenced upon the occasion referred to, for in the prologue Margaret alludes to historical events which took place in 1543 and 1544, and she speaks of them as being of recent occurrence at her time of writing. Now we know that in April 1544 she met her brother at Alençon, and made a long stay in the duchy, and the probability is that she commenced the *Heptameron* at that time. It was the work of several years, penned in a desultory style whilst Margaret was traveling about her northern duchy or her southern kingdom. Like all persons of high station, she journeyed in a litter, and Brantôme informs us that her equipage was a modest one, for "she never had more than three baggage-mules and six for her two litters, though she had two, three, or four chariots for her ladies."[1] Brantôme — who it may be mentioned was brought up at Margaret's Court under the care of his grandmother, Louise de Daillon, wife of Andrew de Vivonne, Seneschal of Poitou — also states that the Queen composed the *Heptameron* mainly "in her litter, while journeying about, for she had more important occupations when she was at home. I have thus heard it related by my grandmother, who always went with her in her litter as her lady of honor, and held the escritoire with which she wrote, and she set them (the stories) down in writing as speedily and skillfully as if they had been dictated to her, if not more so."[2]

In 1545 and 1546 we find Margaret in Beam, whence she addresses New Year epistles to her brother expressing her sorrow at being separated

---

* Henry d'Albret had already undergone treatment at the Pyrenean baths after his escape from Pavia, when, however, he stayed at Eaux-Bonnes.

† Génin's *Nouvelles Lettres, &c.*, p. 189.

‡ A. de Ruble's *Mariage de Jeanne d'Albret*, Paris, 1877, p. 86, et seq.

[1] Lalanne's *Œuvres de Brantôme*, 1875, vol. ii. p. 214.

[2] *Ibid.*, vol. viii. p. 226.

from him. In the spring of the latter year she visits him at Plessis-lès-
Tours. The King of France — contrary to all tradition — enjoys at this
period as good health as the most robust man in his kingdom.* In 1547
Margaret repairs to a convent at Tusson in the Angoumois to spend
Lent there, and soon afterwards is dispatching courier after courier to
the Court at Rambouillet for news of Francis, who is dying. Such is her
anguish of suspense that she exclaims, "Whoever comes to my door to
announce to me the cure of the King my brother, were such a messenger
weary, tired, muddy, and dirty, I would embrace and kiss him like the
cleanest prince and gentleman in France; and if he lacked a bed and
could not find one to repose upon, I would give him mine, and would
sleep on the floor for the sake of the good news he brought me."†

No one, however, had the courage to tell her the truth. It was a poor
maniac who by her tears gave her to understand that the King was no
longer alive. Sainte-Marthe records the incident as follows: "Now the
day that Francis was taken away from us (Margaret herself has since told
me so), she thought whilst sleeping that she saw him looking pale, and
calling for her in a sad voice, which she took for a very evil sign; and
feeling doubtful about it, she sent several messengers to the Court to
ascertain the condition of the King her brother, but not a single one of
them returned to her. One day, her brother having again appeared to
her while she was asleep (he had already been dead fifteen days),‡ she
asked the members of her household if they had heard any news of the
King.

"They replied to her that he was very well, and she then went to the
church. On her way there she summoned Thomas le Coustellier, a young
man of good intelligence and her secretary, and as she was telling him
the substance of a letter that she wished to write to a Princess of the
Court, to obtain from her some news of the King's health, she heard
on the other side of the cloister a nun, whose brain was somewhat
turned, lamenting and weeping loudly. Margaret, naturally inclined to
pity, hastened to this woman, asked her why she was weeping, and
encouraged her to tell her whether she wished for anything. Then the
nun began to lament still more loudly, and looking at the Queen, told
her that she was deploring her ill-fortune. When Margaret heard these
words she turned towards those who were with her, and said to them,
'You were hiding the King's death from me, but the Spirit of God has
revealed it to me through this maniac.' This said, she turned to her

---

* *Lettres de Marguerite, &c.,* p. 473.
† *Œuvres de Brantôme,* 8vo, vol. v. p. 233.
‡ Francis I died March 31, 1547.

room, knelt down, and humbly thanked the Lord for all the goodness He was pleased to show her."*

After losing her brother, Margaret remained in retirement at the convent of Tusson. She stayed there, says Brantôme, for four months, leading a most austere life and discharging the duties of abbess. She still continued in retirement on her return to Beam, mainly occupying herself with literary work. It was in 1547, subsequent to the death of Francis, that John de la Haye, her secretary, published at Lyons her *Marguerites de la Marguerite,* poems which she had composed at various periods, and which De la Haye probably transcribed at her dictation.†

Margaret's daughter Jane was at this period at the Court of France, living in extravagant style, as is shown by the letters in which Margaret declares that the Princess's expenditure is insupportable. She herself spent but little money upon personal needs, though she devoted considerable sums to charity. In October 1548 she emerged from her seclusion to attend the second marriage of her daughter, who now became the wife of Anthony de Bourbon, Duke of Vendôme. From Moulins, where the ceremony took place, Margaret repaired to the Court at Fontainebleau. Here all was changed: there was a new King, and Diana of Poitiers occupied the position of the Duchess of Etampes. After returning to Beam for Christmas, Margaret spent the Lent of 1549 in retreat at Tusson, where she apparently divided her time between prayer and literary labor. She was still writing the *Heptameron,* as is shown by the sixty-sixth tale, which chronicles an adventure that befell her daughter and Anthony de Bourbon on their marriage trip during the winter of 1548–49. It may be noted, too, that the scene of the sixty-ninth story is laid at the Castle of Odos near Tarbes, and as Margaret came to reside at the castle in the autumn of 1549, this tale was probably written during her sojourn there. Whilst adding fresh stories to the *Heptameron,* she was not neglecting poetry, for from this period also dates the *Miroir de Jésus Christ crucifié,* which Brother Olivier published in 1556, stating that it was the Queen's last work, and that she had handed it to him a few days before her death.

Margaret had long been in failing health and was growing extremely weak. Brantôme, on the authority of his grandmother, states that when her approaching death was announced to her, she found the monition a very bitter one, saying that she was not yet so aged but that she might live some years longer. She was then in her fifty-eighth year. Sainte-Marthe relates that shortly before her death she saw in a dream a very

---

* *Oraison funèbre, &c,* p. 103.

† Sainte-Marthe states that she would sit with two secretaries, one on either side, and dictate poetry to the one and letters to the other.

beautiful woman holding in her hand a crown of all sorts of flowers which she showed to her, telling her that she would soon be crowned with it.*

She interpreted this dream as signifying that her end was near, and from that day forward abandoned the administration of her property to the King of Navarre, refusing to occupy herself with any other matter than that of her approaching end. After dictating her will she fell into her final illness, which lasted twenty days according to some authorities, and eight according to others. It seized her one night at Odos whilst she was watching a comet, which it was averred had appeared to notify the death of Pope Paul III. "It was perhaps to presage her own," naïvely remarks Brantôme, who adds that while she was looking at the comet her mouth suddenly became partially paralyzed, whereupon her doctor, M. d'Escuranis, led her away and made her go to bed. Her death took place on December 21st, 1549, and just before expiring she grasped a crucifix that lay beside her and murmured, "Jesus, Jesus, Jesus."†

Although the King of Navarre had not always lived in perfect accord with his wife, he nonetheless keenly felt the loss he had sustained by her death. Olhagaray represents him when deprived of Margaret as no longer showing the same firm purpose of life, but as sad, discontented, and altering his plans at every trifle.‡ He gave orders that Margaret's remains should be interred in the Cathedral of Lescar, some four and a half miles from the Château of Pau, with which it is said to have been at that time connected by a subterranean passage. Several of the Navarrese sovereigns had already been buried there, for the See was a kind of primacy, the Bishops being *ex-officio* presidents of the States of Beam.[1]

It was in this quaint old cathedral church, dating, so archaeologists assert, from the eleventh century, that Margaret's remains were interred with all due pomp and ceremony. The Duchess of Estouteville headed the procession, followed by the Duke of Montpensier, the Duke of Nevers, the Duke of Aumale, the Duke of Etampes, the Marquis of

---

* *Oraison funèbre, &c,* p. 104.

† M. Lalanne, in his edition of Brantôme's works, maintains that Margaret did not die at Odos, near Tarbes, but at Audaux, near Orthez, basing this contention on the fact that Brantôme calls the castle "Audos in Beam," and that Odos is in Bigorre. Tradition, however, has always pointed to the latter locality, though, on the other hand, it is stated that less than half a century after Margaret's death Odos was nothing but a ruin, and had long been in that condition. In 1596 Henry IV gave the property to John de Lassalle, by whose descendants the château was restored (Bascle de Lagrèze's *Château de Pau, &c.*).

‡ *Histoire de Foix et de Béarn, &c.,* p. 506.

[1] Lescar having ceased to be a bishopric since 1790, its church, which still exists, no longer ranks as a cathedral.

Maine, and M. de Rohan. Then came the *grands deuils* or chief mourners, led by the Duke of Vendôme, and three lords carrying the crown, scepter, and hand of justice. The Viscount of Lavedan officiated as grand master of the ceremonies, and special seats were assigned to the States of Navarre, Foix, Beam, and Bigorre, and to the chancellor, counselors, and barons of the country; whilst on a platform surrounded by lighted tapers there was displayed an effigy of the Queen robed in black.* After the ceremony a banquet was served in accordance with Bearnese custom, the chief mourners being invited to the Duke of Vendôme's table, whilst the others were served in different rooms.†

A few years later — in June 1555 — the remains of King Henry, Margaret's husband, were in turn brought to Lescar for burial. The tombs of husband and wife, however, have alike vanished, having been swept away during the religious wars, when Lescar was repeatedly stormed and sacked, when Huguenot and Catholic, in turn triumphant, vented their religious frenzy upon the graves of their former sovereigns; and today the only tombs to be found in the old cathedral are those of personages interred there since the middle of the seventeenth century.

January 1893

---

* *Lettres de Marguerite (Pièces justificatives.* No. xi.).
† Bascle de Lagrèze's *Château de Pau, &c.*

On the Heptameron,

WITH SOME NOTICE OF PRECEDENT COLLECTIONS OF TALES IN FRANCE, OF THE AUTHOR, AND OF HER OTHER WORKS

*I*t is probable that everyone who has had much to do with the study of literature has conceived certain preferences for books which he knows not to belong absolutely to the first order, but which he thinks to have been unjustly depreciated by the general judgment, and which appeal to his own tastes or sympathies with particular strength. One of such books in my own case is *The Heptameron* of Margaret of Navarre. I have read it again and again, sometimes at short intervals, sometimes at longer, during the lapse of some five-and-twenty years since I first met with it. But the place which it holds in my critical judgment and in my private affections has hardly altered at all since the first reading. I like it as a reader perhaps rather more than I esteem it as a critic; but even as a critic, and allowing fully for the personal equation, I think that it deserves a far higher place than is generally accorded to it.

Three mistakes, as it seems to me, pervade most of the estimates, critical or uncritical, of the *Heptameron,* the two first of old date, the third of recent origin. The first is that it is a comparatively feeble imitation of a great original, and that anyone who knows Boccaccio need hardly trouble himself to know Margaret of Navarre. The second is that it is a loose if not obscene book, disgraceful for a lady to have written (or at least mothered), and not very creditable for anyone to read. The third is that it is interesting as the gossip of a certain class of modern newspapers is interesting, because it tells scandal about distinguished personages, and has for its interlocutors other distinguished personages, who can be identified without much difficulty, and the identification of whom adds zest to the reading. All these three seem to me to be mistakes of fact and of judgment. In the first place, the *Heptameron* borrows from its original literally nothing but plan. Its

stories are quite independent; the similarity of name is only a bookseller's invention, though a rather happy one; and the personal setting,
which is in Boccaccio a mere framework, has here considerable substance and interest. In the second place, the accusation of looseness is
wildly exaggerated. There is one very coarse but not in the least immoral
story in the *Heptameron*; there are several broad jests on the obnoxious
cloister and its vices, there are many tales which are not intended
virginibus puerisque, and there is a pervading flavor of that half-French,
half-Italian courtship of married women which was at the time usual
everywhere out of England. The manners are not our manners, and what
may be called the moral tone is distinguished by a singular cast, of which
more presently. But if not entirely a book for boys and girls, the
Heptameron is certainly not one which Southey need have excepted from
his admirable answer in the character of author of "The Doctor," to the
person who wondered whether he (Southey) could have daughters, and
if so, whether they liked reading. "He has daughters: they love reading:
and he is not the man I take him for if they are not 'allowed to open'
any book in his library." The last error, if not so entirely inconsistent
with intelligent reading of the book as the first and second, is scarcely
less strange to me. For, in the first place, the identification of the
personages in the framework of the *Heptameron* depends upon the
merest and, as it seems to me, the idlest conjecture; and, in the second,
the interest of the actual tittle-tattle, whether it could be fathered on A
or B or not, is the least part of the interest of the book. Indeed, the
stories altogether are, as I think, far less interesting than the framework.

Let us see, therefore, if we cannot treat the *Heptameron* in a somewhat
different fashion from that in which any previous critic, even Sainte-
Beuve, has treated it. The divisions of such treatment are not very far
to seek. In the first place, let us give some account of the works of the
same class which preceded and perhaps patterned it. In the second, let
us give an account of the supposed author, of her other works, and of
the probable character of her connection with this one. In the third,
without attempting dry argument, let us give some sketch of the vital
part, which we have called the framework, and some general characteristics of the stories. And, in the fourth and last, let us endeavor to
disengage that peculiar tone, flavor, note, or whatever word may be
preferred, which, as it seems to me at least, at once distinguishes the
Heptameron from other books of the kind, and renders it peculiarly
attractive to those whose temperament and taste predisposes them to
be attracted. For there is a great deal of pre-established harmony in
literature and literary tastes; and I have a kind of idea that every man

has his library marked out for him when he comes into the world, and has then only got to get the books and read them.

Margaret herself refers openly enough to the example of the *Decameron*, which had been translated by her own secretary, Anthony le Maçon, a member of her literary côterie, and not improbably connected with the writing or redacting of the *Heptameron* itself. Nor were later Italian tale-tellers likely to be without influence at a time when French was being "Italianated" in every possible way, to the great disgust of some Frenchmen. But the Italian ancestors or patterns need not be dealt with here, and can be discovered with ease and pleasure by anyone who wishes in the drier pages of Dunlop, or in the more flowery and starry pages of Mr. Symonds' "History of the Renaissance in Italy." The next few pages will deal only with the French tale-tellers, whose productions before Margaret's days were, if not very numerous, far from uninteresting, and whose influence on the slight difference of *genre* which distinguishes the tales before us from Italian tales was by no means slight.

In France, as everywhere else, prose fiction, like prose of all kinds, was considerably later in production than verse, and short tales of the kind before us were especially postponed by the number, excellence, and popularity of the verse *fabliaux*. Of these, large numbers have come down to us, and they exactly correspond in verse to the tales of the *Decameron* and the *Heptameron* in prose, except that the satirical motive is even more strongly marked, and that touches of romantic sentiment are rarer. This element of romance, however, appears abundantly in the long prose versions of the Arthurian and other legends, and we have a certain number of short prose stories of the thirteenth and fourteenth centuries, of which the most famous is that of *Aucassin et Nicolette*. These latter, however, are rather short romances than distinct prose tales of our kind. Of that kind the first famous book in French, and the only famous book, besides the one before us, is the *Cent Nouvelles Nouvelles*. The authorship of this book is very uncertain. It purports to be a collection of stories told by different persons of the society of Louis XI, when he was but Dauphin, and was in exile in Flanders under the protection of the Duke of Burgundy. But it has of late years been very generally assigned (though on rather slender grounds of probability, and none of positive evidence), to Anthony de la Salle, the best French prose writer of the fifteenth century, except Comines, and one on whom, with an odd unanimity, conjectural criticism has bestowed, besides his acknowledged romance of late chivalrous society, *Petit Jehan de Saintré* (a work which itself has some affinities with the class of story before us), not only the *Cent Nouvelles Nouvelles*, but the famous satirical treatise of the *Quinze Joyes du Mariage*, and the still more famous farce of *Pathelin*. Some

of the *Nouvelles,* moreover, have been putatively fathered on Louis XI
himself, in which case the royal house of France would boast of two
distinguished taletellers instead of one. However this may be, they all
display the somewhat hard and grim but keen and practical humor
which seems to have distinguished that prince, which was a characteristic of French thought and temper at the time, and which perhaps
arose with the misfortunes and hardships of the Hundred Years' War.
The stories are decidedly amusing, with a considerably greater, though
also a much ruder, *vis comica* than that of the *Heptameron*; and they are
told in a style unadorned indeed, and somewhat dry, lacking the sim-
plicity of the older French, and not yet attaining to the graces of the
newer, but forcible, distinct, and sculpturesque, if not picturesque. A
great license of subject and language, and an enjoyment of practical
jokes of the roughest, not to say the most cruel character, prevail
throughout, and there is hardly a touch of anything like romance; the
tales alternating between jests as broad as those of the Reeve's and
Miller's tales in Chaucer (themselves exactly corresponding to verse
fabliaux, of which the *Cent Nouvelles* are exact prose counterparts, and
perhaps prose versions), and examples of what has been called "the
humor of the stick," which sometimes trenches hard upon the humor
of the gallows and the torture-chamber. These characteristics have made
the *Cent Nouvelles Nouvelles* no great favorites of late, but their unpopu-
larity is somewhat undeserved. For all their coarseness, there is much
genuine comedy in them, and if the prettiness of romantic and literary
dressing-up is absent from them, so likewise is the insincerity thereof.
They make one of the most considerable prose books of what may be
called middle French literature, and they had much influence on the
books that followed, especially on this of Margaret's. Indeed, one of the
few examples to be found between the two, the *Grand Paragon de
Nouvelles Nouvelles* of Nicolas de Troyes (1535), obviously takes them for
model. But Nicolas was a dull dog, and neither profited by his model
nor gave anyone else opportunity to profit by himself.

Rabelais, the first book of whose *Pantagruel* anticipated the *Paragon*
by three years, while the *Gargantua* coincided with it, was a great
authority at the Court of Margaret's brother Francis, dedicated one of
the books (the third) of *Pantagruel* to her, before her death, in high-flown
language, as *esprit abstrait, ravy et ecstatic,* and must certainly have been
familiar reading of hers, and of all the ladies and gentlemen, literary
and fashionable, of her Court. But there is little resemblance to be found
in his style and hers. The short stories which Master Francis scatters
about his longer work are, indeed, models of narration, but his whole
tone of thought and manner of treatment are altogether alien from those

of the "ravished spirit" whom he praises. His deliberate coarseness is not more different from her deliberate delicacy than his intensely practical spirit from her high-flown romanticism (which makes one think of, and may have suggested, the Court of La Quinte), and her mixture of devout and amatory quodlibetation from his cynical criticism and all-dissolving irony. But there was a contemporary of Rabelais who forms a kind of link between him and Margaret, whose work in part is very like the *Heptameron,* and who has been thought to have had more than a hand in it. This was Bonaventure Despériers, a man whose history is as obscure as his works are interesting. Born in or about the year 1500, he committed suicide in 1544, either during a fit of insanity, or, as has been thought more likely, in order to escape the danger of the persecution which, in the last years of the reign of Francis, threatened the unorthodox, and which Margaret, who had more than once warded it off from them, was then powerless to avert. Despériers, to speak truth, was in far more danger of the stake than most of his friends. The infidelity of Rabelais is a matter of inference only, and some critics (among whom the present writer ranks himself) see in his daring ridicule of existing abuses nothing inconsistent with a perfectly sound, if liberally conditioned, orthodoxy. Despériers, like Rabelais, was a Lucianist, but his modernizing of Lucian (the remarkable book called *Cymbalum Mundï),* though pretending to deal with ancient mythology, has an almost unmistakable reference to revealed religion. It is not, however, by this work or by this side of his character at all that Despériers is brought into connection with the work of Margaret, who, if learned and liberal, and sometimes tending to the new ideas in religion, was always devout and always orthodox in fundamentals. Besides the *Cymbalum Mundi,* he has left a curious book, not published, like the *Heptameron* itself, till long after his own death, and entitled *Nouvelles Récréations et Joyeux Devis.* The tales of which it consists are for the most part very short, some being rather sketches or outlines of tales than actually worked-out stories, so that, although there are no less than a hundred and twenty-nine of them, the whole book is probably not half the bulk of the *Heptameron* itself. But they are extremely well written, and the specially interesting thing about them is, that in them there appears, and appears for the first time (unless we take the *Heptameron* itself as earlier, which is contrary to all probability), the singular and, at any rate to some persons, very attractive mixture of sentiment and satire, of learning and a love of refined society, of joint devotion to heavenly and earthly love, of voluptuous enjoyment of the present, blended and shadowed with a sense of the night that cometh, which delights us in the prose of the *Heptameron,* and in the verse not only of all the Pléiade poets in France, but of Spenser, Donne, and some of their followers in England. The scale of the stories, which are sometimes mere anecdotes, is so small, the room for miscellaneous discourse in them is so scanty, and the absence of any connecting links, such as those of Margaret's own plan, checks the expression of personal feeling so much, that it is only occasionally that this cast of thought can be perceived. But it is there, and its presence is an important element in determining the question of the exact authorship of the *Heptameron* itself.

It can hardly be said that, except translations from the Italian (of which the close intercourse between France and Italy in the days of the later Valois produced many), Margaret had many other examples before her. For such a book as the *Propos Rustiques* of Noël du Fail, though published before her death, is not likely to have exercised any influence over her; and most other books of the kind are later than her own. One such (for, despite its *bizarre* title and its distinct intention of attacking the Roman Church, Henry Estienne's *Apologie pour Hérodote* is really a collection of stories) deserves mention, not because of its influence upon the Queen of Navarre, but because of the Queen of Navarre's influence upon it. Estienne is constantly quoting the *Heptameron,* and though to a certain extent the inveteracy with which the friars are attacked here must have given the book a special attraction for him, two things may be gathered from his quotations and attributions. The first is that the book was a very popular one; the second, that there was no doubt among well-informed persons, of whom and in whose company Estienne most certainly was, that the *Heptameron* was in more than name the work of its supposed author.

From what went before it Margaret could, and could not, borrow certain well-defined things. Models both Italian and French gave her the scheme of including a large number of short and curtly, but not skimpingly, told stories in one general framework, and of subdividing them into groups dealing more or less with the same subject or class of subject. She had also in her predecessors the example of drawing largely on that perennial and somewhat facile source of laughter — the putting together of incidents and phrases which even by those who laugh at them are regarded as indecorous. But of this expedient she availed herself rather less than any of her forerunners. She had further the example of a generally satirical intent; but here, too, she was not content merely to follow, and her satire is, for the most part, limited to the corruptions and abuses of the monastic orders. It can hardly be said that any of the other stock subjects, lawyers, doctors, citizens, even husbands (for she is less satirical on marriage than encomiastic of love), are dealt with much by her. She found also in some, but chiefly in older books of the

Chartier and still earlier traditions, and rather in Italian than in French, a certain strain of romance proper and of adventure; but of this also she availed herself but rarely. What she did not find in any example (unless, and then but partially, in the example of her own servant, Bonaventure Des-périers) was first the interweaving of a great deal not merely of formal religious exercise, but of positive religious devotion in her work; and secondly, the infusing into it of the peculiar Renaissance contrast, so often to be noticed, of love and death, passion and piety, voluptuous enjoyment and somber anticipation.

But it is now time to say a little more about the personality and work of this lady, whose name all this time we have been using freely, and who was indeed a very notable person quite independently of her literary work. Nor was she in literature by any means an unnotable one, quite independently of the collection of unfinished stories, which, after receiving at its first posthumous publication the not particularly appropriate title of *Les Amants Fortunés*, was more fortunately re-named, albeit by something of a bull (for there is the beginning of an eighth day as well as the full complement of the seven), the *Heptameron*.

Few ladies have been known in history by more and more confusing titles than the author of the *Heptameron*, the confusion arising partly from the fact that she had a niece and a great-niece of the same charming Christian name as herself. The second Margaret de Valois (the most appropriate name of all three, as it was theirs by family right) was the daughter of Francis I, the patroness of Ronsard, and, somewhat late in life, the wife of the Duke of Savoy — a marriage which, as the bride carried with her a dowry of territory, was not popular, and brought some coarse jests on her. Not much is said of her personal appearance after her infancy; but she inherited her aunt's literary tastes, if not her literary powers, and gave Ronsard powerful support in his early days. The third was the daughter of Henry II, the "Grosse Margot" of her brother, Henry III, the "Reine Margot" of Dumas' novel, the idol of Brantôme, the first wife of Henry IV, the beloved of Guise, La Mole, and a long succession of gallants, the rival of her sister-in-law Mary Stuart, not in misfortunes, but as the most beautiful, gracious, learned, accomplished, and amiable of the ladies of her time. This Margaret would have been an almost perfect heroine of romance (for she had every good quality except chastity), if she had not unluckily lived rather too long.

Her great-aunt, our present subject, was not the equal of her great-niece in beauty, her portraits being rendered uncomely by a portentously long nose, longer even than Mrs. Siddons's, and by a very curious expression of the eyes, going near to slyness. But the face is one which can be imagined as much more beautiful than it seems in the not very attractive portraiture of the time, and her actual attractions are attested by her contemporaries with something more than the homage-to-order which literary men have never failed to pay to ladies who are patronesses of letters. Besides Margaret of Valois, she is known as Margaret of Angoulême, from her place of birth and her father's title; Margaret of Alençon, from the fief of her first husband; Margaret of Navarre, of which country, like her grand-niece, she was queen, by her second marriage with Henry d'Albret; and even Margaret of Orleans, as belonging to the Orleans branch of the royal house. She was not, like her nieces, Margaret of France, as her father never reigned, and Brantôme properly denies her the title, but others sometimes give it. When it is necessary to call her anything besides the simple "Margaret," Angoulême is at once the most appropriate and the most distinctive designation. She was born on the 11th or 12th of April 1492, her father being Charles, Count of Angoulême, and her mother Louise of Savoy. She was their eldest child, and two years older than her brother, the future King Francis. According to, and even in excess of, the custom of the age, she received a very learned education, acquiring not merely the three tongues, French, Italian, and Spanish, which were all in common use at the French Court during her time, but Latin, and even a little Greek and a little Hebrew. She lived in the provinces both before and after her marriage, in 1509, to her relation, Charles, Duke of Alençon, who was older than herself by three years, and though a fair soldier and an inoffensive person, was apparently of little talents and not particularly amiable. The accession of her brother to the throne opened a much more brilliant career to her. She and her mother jointly exercised great influence over Francis; and the Duchess of Alençon, to whom her brother shortly afterwards gave Berry, was for many years one of the most influential persons in the kingdom, using her influence almost invariably for good. Her husband died soon after Pavia, and in the same year (September 1525) she undertook a journey to Spain on behalf of her captive brother. This journey, with some expressions in her letters and in Brantôme, has been wrested by some critics in order to prove that her affection for Francis was warmer than it ought to have been — an imputation wanton in both senses of the word.

She was sought in marriage by or offered in marriage to divers distinguished persons during her widowhood, and this was also the time of her principal diplomatic exercise, an office for which — odd as it now seems for a woman — she had, like her mother, like her niece Catherine of Medicis, like her namesake Margaret of Parma, and like other ladies of the age, a very considerable aptitude and reputation. When she at last married, the match was not a brilliant one, though it proved, contrary to immediate probability, to be the source of the last and the most glorious branch of the royal dynasty of France. The bridegroom bore indeed the title of King of Navarre and possessed Beam, but his kingdom had long been in Spanish hands, and but for his wife's dowry of Alençon and appanage of Berry (to which Francis had added Armagnac and a large pension) he would have been but a lackland. Furthermore, he was eleven years younger than herself, and it is at least insinuated that the affection, if there was any, was chiefly on her side. At any rate, this earlier Henry of Navarre seems to have had not a few of the characteristics of his grandson, together with a violence and brutality which, to do the *Vert Galant* justice, formed no part of his character. The only son of the marriage died young, and a girl, Jane d'Albret, mother of the great Bourbon race of the next two centuries, was taken away from her parents by "reasons of state" for a time. The domestic life of Margaret, however, concerns us but little, except in one way. Her husband disliked administration, and she was the principal ruler in their rather extensive estates or dominions. Moreover, she was able at her quasi-Court to extend the literary côteries which she had already begun to form at Paris. The patronage to men of letters for which her brother is famous was certainly more due to her than to himself; and to her also was due the partial toleration of religious liberty which for a time distinguished his reign. It was not till her influence was weakened that intolerance prevailed, and she was able even then for a time to save Marot and other distinguished persons from persecution. It is rather a moot-point how far she inclined to the Reformed doctrines, properly so called. Her letters, her serious and poetical work, and even the *Heptameron* itself, show a fervently pietistic spirit, and occasionally seem to testify to a distinct inclination towards Protestantism, which is also positively attested by Brantôme and others; but this Protestantism must have been, so far as it was consistent and definite at all, the Protestantism of Erasmus rather than of Luther, of Rabelais rather than of Calvin. She had a very strong objection to the coarseness, the vices, the idleness, the brutish ignorance of the cloister; she had aspirations after a more spiritual form of religion than the ordinary Catholicism of her day provided, and as a strong politician she may have had something of that Gallicanism which has always been well marked in some of the best Frenchmen, and which at one time nearly prevailed with her great-great-grandson, Louis XIV. But there is no doubt that, as her brother said to the fanatical Montmorency, she would always have been and always was of his religion, the religion of the State. The side of the Reformation which must have most appealed to her was neither its austere morals, nor its bare ritual, nor its doctrines, properly so called, but its spiritual pietism and its connection with profane learning and letters; for of literature Margaret was an ardent devotee and a constant practitioner.

Her best days were done by the time of her second marriage. After the King's return from Spain persecution broke out, and Margaret's influence became more and more weak to stop it. As early as 1533 her own *Miroir de l'Ame Pécheresse,* then in a second edition, provoked the fanaticism of the Sorbonne, and the King had to interfere in person to protect his sister's work and herself from gross insult. The Medici marriage increased the persecuting tendency, and for a time there was even an attempt to suppress printing, and with it all that new literature which was the Queen's delight. She was herself in some danger, but Francis had not sunk so low as to permit any actual attack to be made on her. Yet all the last years of her life were unhappy, though she continued to keep Court at Nérac in Pau, to accompany her brother in his progresses, and, as we know from documents, to play Lady Bountiful over a wide area of France. Her husband appears to have been rather at variance with her; and her daughter, who married first, and in name only, the Duke of Cleves in 1540, and later (1548) Anthony de Bourbon, was also not on cordial terms with her mother. By the date of this second marriage Francis was dead, and though he had for many years been anything but wholly kind, Margaret's good days were now in truth done. Her nephew Henry left her in possession of her revenues, but does not seem to have been very affectionately disposed towards her; and even had she been inclined to attempt any recovery of influence, his wife and his mistress, Catherine de Medici and Diana of Poitiers, two women as different from Margaret as they were from one another, would certainly have prevented her from obtaining it. As a matter of fact, however, she had long been in ill-health, and her brother's death seems to have dealt her the final stroke. She survived it two years, even as she had been born two years before him, and died on the 21st December 1549, at the Castle of Odos, near Tarbes, having lived in almost complete retirement for a considerable time. Her husband is said to have regretted her dead more than he loved her living, and her literary admirers, such of them as death and exile had spared, were not ungrateful. *Tombeaux,* or collections of funeral verses, were not lacking, the first being in Latin, and, oddly enough, nominally by three English sisters, Anne, Margaret, and Jane Seymour, nieces of Henry VIII's queen and Edward VI's mother, with learned persons like Dorât, Sainte-Marthe, and Baïf. This was re-issued in French and in a fuller form later.

Some reference has been made to an atrocious slur cast without a shred of evidence on her moral character. There is as little foundation for more general though milder charges of laxity. It is admitted that she had little love for her first husband, and it seems to be probable that her second had not much love for her. She was certainly addressed in gallant strains by men of letters, the most audacious being Clement Marot; but the almost universal reference of the well-known and delightful lines beginning —

"Un doux nenny avec un doux sourire,"

to her method of dealing not merely with this lover but with others, argues a general confidence in her being a virtuous coquette, if somewhat coquettishly virtuous. It may be added that the whole tone of the *Heptameron* points to a very similar conclusion.

Her literary work was very considerable, and it falls under three divisions: letters, the book before us, and the very curious and interesting collection of poems known by the charming if fantastic title of *Les Marguerites de la Marguerite des Princesses*, a play on the meanings, daisy, pearl, and Margaret, which had been popular in the artificial school of French poetry since the end of the thirteenth century in a vast number of forms.

The letters are naturally of the very first importance for determining the character of Margaret's life as a woman of business, a diplomatist, and so forth. They show her to us in all these capacities, and also in that of an enlightened and always ready patroness of letters and of men of letters. Further, they are of value, though their value is somewhat affected by a reservation to be made immediately, as to her mental and moral characteristics. But they are not of literary interest at all equal to that of either of the other divisions. They are, if not spoilt, still not improved, by the fact that the art of easy letter-writing, in which Frenchwomen of the next century were to show themselves such proficients, had not yet been developed, and that most of them are couched in a heavy, laborious, semiofficial style, which smells, as far as mere style goes, of the cumbrous refinements of the *rhétoriqueurs*, in whose flourishing time Margaret herself grew up, and which conceals the writer's sentiments under elaborate forms of ceremonial courtesy. Something at least of the groundless scandal before referred to is derived in all probability, if not in all certainty, from the lavish use of hyperbole in addressing her brother; and generally speaking, the rebuke of the Queen to Polonius, "More matter with less art," is applicable to the whole correspondence.

Something of the same evil influence is shown in the Marguerites. It must be remembered that the writer died before the Pléiade movement had been fully started, and that she was older by five years than Marot, the only one of her own contemporaries and her own literary circle who attained to a poetic style easier, freer, and more genuine than the

cumbrous rhetoric, partly derived from the allegorizing style of the
Roman de la Rose and its followers, partly influenced by corrupt following of the re-discovered and scarcely yet understood classics, partly
alloyed with Flemish and German and Spanish stiffness, of which
Chastellain, Crétin, and the rest have been the frequently quoted and
the rarely read exponents to students of French literature. The contents
of the *Marguerites,* to take the order of the beautiful edition of M. Félix
Frank, are as follows: Volume I contains first a long and singular
religious poem entitled *Le Miroir de l'Ame Pécheresse,* in rhymed decasyl-
lables, in which pretty literal paraphrases of a large number of passages
of Scripture are strung together with a certain amount of pious com-
ment and reflection. This is followed (after a shorter piece on the contest
in the human soul between the laws of the spirit and of the flesh) by
another poem of about the same length as the *Miroir,* and of no very
different character, entitled *Oraison de L'Ame Fidèle à son Seigneur Dieu,*
and a shorter *Oraison à Notre Seigneur Jésus Christ* completes the volume.
The second volume yields four so-called "comedies," but really mysteries
on the old mediæval model, only distinguishable from their forerunners
by slightly more modern language and a more scriptural tone. The
subjects are the Nativity, the Adoration of the Three Kings, the Massacre
of the Innocents, and the Flight into Egypt. The third volume contains
a third poem in the style of the *Miroir,* but much superior, *Le Triomphe
de l'Agneau,* a considerable body of spiritual songs, a miscellaneous poem
or two, and some epistles, chiefly addressed to Francis. These last begin
the smaller and secular division of the *Marguerites,* which is completed
in the fourth volume by *Les Quatre Dames et les Quatre Gentilhommes,*
composed of long monologues after the fashion of the Froissart-Char-
tier school, by a *"comédie profane,"* a farce entitled *Trop, Prou [much], Peu,
Moins*; a long love poem, again in the Chartier style, entitled *La Coche,*
and some minor pieces.

Opinion as to these poems has varied somewhat, but their merit has
never been put very high, nor, to tell the truth, could it be put high by
anyone who speaks critically. In the first place, they are written for the
most part on very bad models, both in general plan and in particular
style and expression. The plan is, as has been said, taken from the
long-winded allegorical erotic poetry of the very late thirteenth, the
fourteenth, and the fifteenth centuries — poetry which is now among
the most difficult to read in any literature. The groundwork or canvas
being transferred from love to religion, it gains a little in freshness and
directness of purpose, but hardly in general readableness. Thus, for
instance, two whole pages of the *Miroir,* or some forty or fifty lines, are
taken up with endless playings on the words *mort* and *vie* and their

derivatives, such as *mortifiez, and mort fiez, mort vivifiée and vie mourante.* The sacred comedies or mysteries have the tediousness and lack of action of the older pieces of the same kind without their *naïveté*; and pretty much the same may be said of the profane comedy (which is a kind of morality), and of the farce. Of *La Coche,* what has been said of the long sacred poems may be said, except that here we go back to the actual subject of the models, not on the whole with advantage: while in the minor pieces the same word plays and frigid conceits are observable.

But if this somewhat severe judgment must be passed on the poems as wholes, and from a certain point of view, it may be considerably softened when they are considered more in detail. In not a few passages of the religious poems Margaret has reached (and as she had no examples before her except Marot's psalms, which were themselves later than at least some of her work, may be said to have anticipated) that grave and solemn harmony of the French Huguenots of the sixteenth century, which in Du Bartas, in Agrippa d'Aubigné, and in passages of the tragedian Montchrestien, strikes notes hardly touched elsewhere in French literature. The *Triomphe de l'Agneau* displays her at her best in this respect, and not infrequently comes not too far off from the apocalyptic resonance of d'Aubigné himself. Again, the *Bergerie* included in the Nativity comedy or mystery, though something of a Dresden *Bergerie* (to use a later image), is graceful and elegant enough in all conscience. But it is on the minor poems, especially the Epistles and the *Chansons Spirituelles,* that the defenders of Margaret's claim to be a poet rest most strongly. In the former her love, not merely for her brother, but for her husband, appears unmistakably, and suggests graceful thoughts. In the latter the force and fire which occasionally break through the stiff wrappings of the longer poems appear with less difficulty and in fuller measure.

It is, however, undoubtedly curious, and not to be explained merely by the difference of subject, that the styles of the letters and of the poems, agreeing well enough between themselves, differ most remarkably from that of the *Heptameron.* The two former are decidedly open to the charges of pedantry, artificiality, heaviness. There is a great surplusage of words and a seeming inability to get to the point. The *Heptameron* if not equal in narrative vigor and lightness to Boccaccio before and La Fontaine afterwards, is not in the least exposed to the charge of clumsiness of any kind, employs a simple, natural, and sufficiently picturesque vocabulary, avoids all verbiage and roundabout writing, and both in the narratives and in the connecting conversation displays a very considerable advance upon nearly all the writers of the time, except Rabelais, Marot, and Despériers, in easy command of the vernacular. It is, therefore, not wonderful that there has, at different times (rather less of late years, but that is probably an accident), been a disposition if not to take away from Margaret all the credit of the book, at any rate to give a share of it to others. In so far as this share is attempted to be bestowed on ladies and gentlemen of her Court or family there is very little evidence for it; but in so far as the pen may be thought to have been sometimes held for her by the distinguished men of letters just referred to (there is no reason why Master Francis himself should not have sometimes guided it), and by others only less distinguished, there is considerable internal reason to favor the idea. At all times and in all places — in France perhaps more than anywhere else — kings and queens, lords and ladies, have found no difficulty (we need not use the harsh Voltairian-Carlylian phrase, and say in getting their literary work "buckwashed," but) in getting it pointed and seasoned, trimmed and ornamented by professional men of letters. The form of the *Heptameron* lends itself more than any other to such assistance; and while I should imagine that the setting, with its strong color, both of religiosity and amorousness, is almost wholly Margaret's work, I should also think it so likely as to be nearly certain that in some at least of the tales the hands of the authors of the *Cymbalum Mundi* and the *Adolescence Clémentine,* of Le Maçon and Brodeau, may have worked at the devising, very likely re-shaped and adjusted by the Queen herself, of the actual stories as we have them now.

The book, as we have it, consists of seven complete days of ten novels each, and of an eighth containing two novels only. The fictitious scheme of the setting is somewhat less lugubrious than that of the *Decameron,* but still not without an element of tragedy. On the first of September, "when the hot springs of the Pyrenees begin to enter upon their virtue," a company of persons of quality assembled at Cauterets, we are told, and abode there three weeks with much profit. But when they tried to return, rain set in with such severity that they thought the Deluge had come again, and they found their roads, especially that to the French side, almost entirely barred by the Gave de Béarn and other rivers. So they scattered in different directions, most of them taking the Spanish side, either along the mountains and across to Roussillon or straight to Barcelona, and thence home by sea. But a certain widow, named Oisille, made her way with much loss of men and horses to the Abbey of Notre Dame de Serrance. Here she was joined by divers gentlemen and ladies, who had had even worse experiences of travel than herself, with bears and brigands, and other evil things, so that one of them, Longarine, had lost her husband, murdered in an affray in one of the cutthroat inns always dear to romance. Besides this disconsolate person and Oisille, the company consisted of a married pair, Hircan and Parlamente; two young cavaliers, Dagoucin and Saffredent; two young ladies, Nomerfide and Ennasuite; Simontault, a cavalier-servant of Parlamente; and Geburon, a knight older and discreeter than the rest of the company except Oisille.*

These form the party, and it is to be noted that idle and contradictory as all the attempts made to identify them have been (for instance, the most confident interpreters hesitate between Oisille and Parlamente, an aged widow and a youthful wife, for Margaret herself), it is not to be denied that the various parts are kept up with much decision and spirit. Of the men, indeed, Hircan is the only one who has a very decided character, and is represented as fond of his wife, Parlamente, but a decided libertine and of a somewhat rough and ruthless general character – points which have made the interpreters sure that he must be Henry d'Albret. The others, except that Geburon is, as had been said, older than his companions, and that Simontault sighs vainly after Parlamente, are merely walking gentlemen of the time, accomplished enough, but not individual. The women are much more distinct and show a woman's hand. Oisille is, as our own seventeenth-century ancestors would have said, ancient and sober, very devout, regarded with great respect by the rest of the company, and accepted as a kind of mistress both of the revels and of more serious matters, but still a woman of the world, and content to make only an occasional and mild protest against tolerably free stories and sentiments. Parlamente, considerably younger, and though virtuous, not by any means ignorant of or wholly averse to the devotion of Simontault, indulging occasionally in a kind of mild conjugal sparring with her husband, Hircan, but apparently devoted to him, full of religion and romance and refinement at once, is a very charming character, resembling Madame de Sévigné as she may have been in her unknown or hardly known youth, when husband and lovers alike were attracted by the flame of her beauty and charm, only to complain that it froze and did not burn. Longarine is discreetly unhappy for her dead husband, but appears decidedly consolable; Ennasuite is a haughty damsel, disdainful of poor folk, and Nomerfide is a pure madcap, a Catherine Seyton of the generation before Catherine herself, the feminine Dioneo of the party, and, if a little too free-spoken for prudish modern taste, a very delightful girl.

Now when this good company had assembled at Serrance and told each other their misadventures, the waters on inquiry seemed to be out more widely and more dangerously than before, so that it was impossible

* These names have been accommodated to M. Le Roux de Lincy's orthography, from MS. No. 1512; but for myself I prefer the spellings, especially "Emarsuitte," more usual in the printed editions. – G. S.

to think of going farther for the time. They deliberated accordingly how they should employ themselves, and, after allowing, on the proposal of Oisille, an ample space for sacred exercises, they resolved that every day, after dinner and an interval, they should assemble in a meadow on the bank of the Gave at midday and tell stories. The device is carried out with such success that the monks steal behind the hedges to hear them, and an occasional postponement of vespers takes place. Simontault begins, and the system of tale-telling goes round on the usual plan of each speaker naming him or her who shall follow. It should be observed that no general subject is, as in the *Decameron,* prescribed to the speakers of each day, though, as a matter of course, one subject often suggests another of not dissimilar kind. Nor is there the Decameronic arrangement of the "king." Between the stories, and also between the days, there is often a good deal of conversation, in which the divers characters, as given above, are carried out with a minuteness very different from the chief Italian original.

From what has been said already, it will be readily perceived that the novels, or rather their subjects, are not very easy to class in any rationalized order. The great majority, if they do not answer exactly to the old title of *Les Histoires des Amants Fortunés,* are devoted to the eternal subject of the tricks played by wives to the disadvantage of husbands, by husbands to the disadvantage of wives, and sometimes by lovers to the disadvantage of both. "Subtilité" is a frequent word in the titles, and it corresponds to a real thing. Another large division, trenching somewhat upon the first, is composed of stories to the discredit of the monks (something, though less, is said against the secular clergy), and especially of the Cordeliers or Franciscans, an Order who, for their coarse immorality and their brutal antipathy to learning, were the special black (or rather grey) beasts of the literary reformers of the time. In a considerable number there are references to actual personages of the time — references which stand on a very different footing of identification from the puerile guessings at the personality of the interlocutors so often referred to. Sometimes these references are avowed: "Un des muletiers de la Reine de Navarre," "Le Roi François montre sa générosité," "Un Président de Grenoble," "Une femme d'Alençon," and so forth. At other times the reference is somewhat more covert, but hardly to be doubted, as in the remarkable story of a "great Prince" (obviously Francis himself) who used on his journeyings to and from an assignation of a very illegitimate character, to turn into a church and piously pursue his devotions. There are a few curious stories in which amatory matters play only a subordinate part or none at all, though it must be confessed that this last is a rare thing. Some are mere anecdote plays on words (sometimes pretty free, and then generally told by Nomer-fide), or quasi-historical, such as that already noticed of the generosity of Francis to a traitor, or deal with remarkable trials and crimes, or merely miscellaneous matters, the best of the last class being the capital "Bonne invention pour chasser le lutin."

In so large a number of stories with so great a variety of subjects, it naturally cannot but be the case that there is a considerable diversity of tone. But that peculiarity at which we have glanced more than once, the combination of voluptuous passion with passionate regret and a mystical devotion, is seldom absent for long together. The general note, indeed, of the *Heptameron* is given by more than one passage in Brantôme — at greatest length by one which Sainte-Beuve has rightly quoted, at the same time and also rightly rebuking the skeptical Abbé's determination to see in it little more than a piece of *précieuse* mannerliness (though, indeed, the *Précieuses* were not yet). Yet even Sainte-Beuve has scarcely pointed out quite strongly enough how entirely this is the keynote of all Margaret's work, and especially of the *Heptameron*. The story therefore may be worth telling again, though it may be found in the "Cinquième Discours" of the *Vies des Dames Galantes*.

Brantôme's brother, not yet a captain in the army, but a student traveling in Italy, had in sojourning at Ferrara, when Renée of France was Duchess, fallen in love with a certain Mademoiselle de la Roche. For love of him she had returned to France, and, visiting his own country of Gasçony, had attached herself to the Court of Margaret, where she had died. And it happened that Bourdeilles, six months afterwards, and having forgotten all about his dead love, came to Pau and went to pay his respects to the Queen. He met her coming back from vespers, and she greeted him graciously, and they talked of this matter and of that. But, as they walked together hither and thither, the Queen drew him, without cause shown, into the church she had just left, where Mademoiselle de la Roche was buried. "Cousin," said she, "do you feel nothing stirring beneath you and under your feet?" But he said, "Nothing, Madame." "Think, cousin," then said she once again. But he said, "Madame, I have thought well, but I feel naught; for under me there is but a stone, hard and firmly set." "Now, do I tell you," said the Queen, leaving him no longer at study, "that you are above the tomb and the body of Mademoiselle de la Roche, who is buried beneath you, and whom you loved so much in her lifetime. And since our souls have sense after our death, it cannot be but that this faithful one, dead so lately, felt your presence as soon as you came near her; and if you have not perceived it, because of the thickness of the tomb, doubt not that nonetheless she felt it. And forasmuch as it is a pious work to make memory of the dead, and notably of those whom we loved, I pray you give her a *pater* and an *ave*, and likewise a *de profundis*, and pour out holy water. So shall you make acquist of the name of a right faithful lover and a good Christian." And she left him that he might do this.

Brantôme (though he had an admiration for Margaret, whose lady of honor his grandmother had been, and who, according to the Bourdeilles tradition, composed her novels in traveling) thought this a pretty fashion of converse. "Voilà," he says, "l'opinion de cette bonne princesse; laquelle la tenait plus par gentillesse et par forme de devis que par créance à mon avis." Sainte-Beuve, on the contrary, and with better reason, sees in it faith, graciousness, feminine delicacy, and piety at once. No doubt; but there is something more than this, and that something more is what we are in search of, and what we shall find, now in one way, now in another, throughout the book: something whereof the sentiment of Donne's famous thoughts on the old lover's ghost, on the blanched bone with its circlet of golden tresses, is the best known instance in English. The madcap Nomerfide indeed lays it down, that "the meditation of death cools the heart not a little." But her more experienced companions know better. The worse side of this Renaissance peculiarity is told in the last tale, a rather ghastly story of monkish corruption; its lighter side appears in the story, already referred to, of the "Grand Prince" and his pious devotions on the way to not particularly pious occupation. But touches of the more poetical and romantic effects of it are all over the book. It is to be found in the story of the gentleman who forsook the world because of his beloved's cruelty, whereat she repenting did likewise ("he had much better have thrown away his cowl and married her," quoth the practical Nomerfide); in that of the wife who, to obtain freedom of living with her paramour, actually allowed herself to be buried; in that (very characteristic of the time, especially for the touch of farce in it) of the unlucky person to whom phlebotomy and love together were fatal; and in not a few others, while it emerges in casual phrases of the intermediate conversations and of the stories themselves, even when it is not to be detected in the general character of the subjects.

And thus we can pretty well decide what is the most interesting and important part of the whole subject. The question, What is the special virtue of the *Heptameron?* I have myself little hesitation in answering. There is no book, in prose and of so early a date, which shows to me the characteristic of the time as it influenced the two great literary nations of Europe so distinctly as this book of Margaret of Angoulême. Take it as a book of Court gossip, and it is rather less interesting than most books of Court gossip, which is saying much. Take it as the performance of a single person, and you are confronted with the difficulty that it is quite unlike that other person's more certain works, and that it is in all probability a joint affair. Take its separate stories, and, with rare exceptions, they are not of the first order of interest, or even of the second. But separate the individual purport of these stories from the general color or tone of them; take this general color or tone in connection with the tenor of the intermediate conversations, which form so striking a characteristic of the book, and something quite different appears. It is that same peculiarity which appears in places and persons and things so different as Spenser, as the poetry of the Pléiade, as Montaigne, as Raleigh, as Donne, as the group of singers known as the Caroline poets. It is a peculiarity which has shown itself in different forms at different times, but never in such vigor and precision as at this time. It combines a profound and certainly sincere – almost severe – religiosity with a very vigorous practice of some things which the religion it professes does not at all countenance. It has an almost morbidly pronounced simultaneous sense of the joys and the sorrows of human life, the enjoyment of the joys being perfectly frank, and the feeling of the sorrows not in the least sentimental. It unites a great general refinement of thought, manners, opinion, with an almost astonishing occasional coarseness of opinion, manners, thought. The prevailing note in it is a profound melancholy mixed with flashes and intervals of a no less profound delight. There is in it the sense of death, to a strange and, at first sight, almost unintelligible extent. Only when one remembers the long night of the religious wars which was just about to fall on France, just as after Spenser, Puritan as he was, after Carew and Herrick still more, a night of a similar character was about to fall on England, does the real reason of this singular idiosyncrasy appear. The company of the *Heptameron* are the latest representatives, at first hand, and with no deliberate purpose of presentment, of the mediaeval conception of gentlemen and ladies who fleeted the time goldenly. They are not themselves any longer mediaeval; they have been taught modern ways; they have a kind of uneasy sense (even though one and another of themselves may now and then flout the idea) of the importance of other classes, even of some duty on their own part towards other classes. Their piety is a very little deliberate, their voluptuous indulgence has a grain of conscience in it and behind it, which distinguishes it not less from the frank indulgence of a Greek or a Roman than from the still franker naïveté of purely mediaeval art, from the childlike, almost paradisiac, innocence of the Belli-cents and Nicolettes and of the daughter of the great Soldan Hugh in that wonderful seriocomic *chanson* of the *Voyage à Constantinople*. The mark of modernity is on them, and yet they are so little conscious of it, and so perfectly free from even the slightest touch of at least its anti-religious influence. Nobody, not even Hircan, the Grammont of the sixteenth century; not even Nomerfide, the Miss Notable of her day and society; not even the haughty lady Ennasuite, who wonders whether common folk can be supposed to have like passions with us, feels the abundant religious services and the periods of meditation unconscionable or tiresome.

And so we have here three notes constantly sounding together or in immediate sequence. There is the passion of that exquisite *rondeau* of Marot's, which some will have, perhaps not impossibly, to refer to Margaret herself —

En la baisant m'a dit: "Amy sans blasme,
Ce seul baiser, qui deux bouches embasme,
Les arrhes sont du bien tant espéré,"
Ce mot elle a doulcement proféré,
Pensant du tout apaiser ma grand flamme.
Mais le mien cour adonc plus elle enflamme,
Car son alaine odorant plus que basme
Souffloit le feu qu'Amour m'a préparé,
En la baisant.

Bref, mon esprit, sans congnoissance d'âme,
Vivoit alors sur la bouche à ma dame,
Dont se mouroit le corps énamouré;
Et si la lèvre eust guères demouré
Contre la mienne, elle m'eust succé l'âme,
En la baisant.

There is the devout meditation of Oisille, and that familiarity with the Scriptures which, as Hircan himself says, "I trow we all read and know." And then there is the note given by two other curious stories of Brantôme. One tells how the Queen of Navarre watched earnestly for hours by the bedside of a dying maid of honor, that she might see whether the parting of the soul was a visible fact or not. The second tells how when some talked before her of the joys of heaven, she sighed and said, "Well, I know that this is true; but we dwell so long dead underground before we arise thither." There, in a few words, is the secret of *The Heptameron*: the fear of God, the sense of death, the voluptuous longing and voluptuous regret for the good things of life and love that pass away.

GEORGE SAINTSBURY[*]

LONDON, *October 1892*

---

†† As I have spoken so strongly of the attempts to identify the personages of the *Heptameron,* it might seem discourteous not to mention that one of the most enthusiastic and erudite English students of Margaret, Madame Darmesteter (Miss Mary Robinson), appears to be convinced of the possibility and advisableness of discovering these originals. Everything that this lady writes is most agreeable to read; but I fear I cannot say that her arguments have converted me. – G. S.

Dedications and Preface,

PREFIXED TO THE FIRST TWO EDITIONS OF THE TALES OF THE QUEEN OF NAVARRE

To the most Illustrious, most Humble, and most Excellent Princess,
Madame Margaret de Bourbon,
  Duchess of Nevers, Marchioness of Illes, Countess of Eu, of Dreux, Rételois, Columbiers, and Beaufort, Lady of Aspremont, of Cham-Regnault, of Arches, Rencaurt, Monrond, and La Chapelle-d'Angylon, Peter Boaistuau surnamed Launay, offers most humble salutation and perpetual obedience.*

  Madam, That great oracle of God, St. John Chrysostom, deplores with infinite compassion in some part of his works the disaster and calamity of his century, in which not only was the memory of an infinity of illustrious persons cut off from among mankind, but, what is more, their writings, by which the rich conceptions of their souls and the divine ornaments of their minds were to have been consecrated to posterity, did not survive them. And certainly with most manifest reason did this good and holy man address such a complaint to the whole Christian Republic, touched as he was with just grief for an infinity of thousands of books, of which some have been lost and buried in eternal forgetfulness by the negligence of men, others dispersed and destroyed by the cruel incursions of war, others rotted and spoiled as much by the rigor of time as by carelessness to collect and preserve them; whereof the ancient Histories and Annals furnish a sufficient example in the memorable library of that great King of Egypt, Ptolemy Phila-delphus, which had been formed with the sweat and blood of so many notable

---

* This dedicatory preface appeared in the first edition of Queen Margaret's Tales, published by Boaistuau in 1558 under the title of *Histoires des Amans Fortunez.* The Princess addressed was the daughter of Charles, Duke of Vendôme; she was wedded in 1538 to Francis of Cleves, Duke of Nevers, and by this marriage became niece to the Queen of Navarre. — Ed.

philosophers, and maintained, ordered, and preserved by the liberality
of that great monarch. And yet in less than a day, by the monstrous and
abominable cruelty of the soldiers of Cæsar, when the latter followed
Pompey to Alexandria, it was burned and reduced to ashes. Zonarius,
the ecclesiastical historian, writes that the same happened at Constantinople in the time of Zeno, when a superb and magnificent palace,
adorned with all sorts of manuscript books, was burned, to the eternal
regret and insupportable detriment of all those who made a profession
of letters. And without amusing ourselves too curiously in recounting
the destruction among the ancients, we have in our time experienced a
similar loss — of which the memory is so recent that the wounds thereof
still bleed in all parts of Europe — namely, when the Turks besieged
Buda, the capital of Hungary, where the most celebrated library of the
good King Matthias was pillaged, dispersed, and destroyed; a library
which, without sparing any expense, he had enriched with all the rarest
and most excellent books, Greek, Latin, Hebrew, and Arabic, that he
had been able to collect in all the most famous provinces of the earth.

Again, he who would particularize and closely examine things will
find that Theophrastes, as he himself declares, wrote and composed three
hundred volumes, Chrysippus sixty, Empedocles fifty, Servus Sulpicius
two hundred on civil law, Gallienus one hundred and thirty on the art
of medicine, and Origenes six thousand, all of which St. Jerome attests
having read; and yet, of so many admirable and excellent authors, there
now remain to us only some little fragments, so debased and vitiated
in several places, that they seem abortive, and as if they had been torn
from their author's hands by force.

On account of which, my Lady, since the occasion has offered, I have
been minded to present all these examples, with the object of exhorting
all those who treasure books and keep them sequestered in their sanc-
tuaries and cabinets, to henceforth publish them and bring them to
light, not only so that they may not keep back and bury the glory of
their ancestors, but also that they may not deprive their descendants of
the profit and pleasure which they might derive from the labor of others.

In regard to myself, I will set forth more amply in the notice which
I will give to the reader the motive that induced me to put my hand to
the work of the present author, who has no need of trumpet and herald
to exalt and magnify her* greatness, inasmuch as there is no human
eloquence that could portray her more forcibly than she has portrayed

---

* In the French text Boaistuau invariably refers to the author as a personage of the
masculine sex, with the evident object of concealing the real authorship of the work.
Feminine pronouns have, however, been substituted in the translation, as it is Queen
Margaret who is referred to. — Ed.

herself by the celestial strokes of her own brush; I mean by her other writings, in which she has so well expressed the sincerity of her doctrines, the vivacity of her faith, and the uprightness of her morals, that the most learned men who reigned in her time were not ashamed to call her a prodigy and miracle of nature. And albeit that Heaven, jealous of our welfare, has snatched her from this mortal habitation, yet her virtues rendered her so admirable and so engraved her in the memory of everyone, that the injury and lapse of time cannot efface her from it; for we shall ceaselessly mourn and lament for her, like Antimachus the Greek poet wept for Lysidichea, his wife, with sad verses and delicate elegies which describe and reveal, her virtues and merits.

Therefore, my Lady, as this work is about to be exposed to the doubtful judgment of so many thousands of men, may it please you to take it under your protection and into your safe keeping; for, whereas you are the natural and legitimate heiress of all the excellencies, ornaments, and virtues which enriched the author while she adorned by her presence the surprise of the earth, and which now by some marvelous ray of divinity live and display themselves in you, it is not possible that you should be defrauded of the fruit of the labor which justly belongs to you, and for which the whole universe will be indebted to you now that it comes forth into the light under the resplendent shelter of your divine and heroic virtues.

May it therefore please you, my Lady, to graciously accept of this little offering, as an eternal proof of my obedience and most humble devotion to your greatness, pending a more important sacrifice which I prepare for the future.

Peter Boaistuau, surnamed Launay, To the Reader*

Gentle Reader,

I can tell thee verily and with good right assert (even prove by witnesses worthy of belief) when this work was presented to me that I might fulfill the office of a sponge and cleanse it of a multitude of manifest errors that were found in a copy written by hand, I was only requested to take out or copy eighteen or twenty of the more notable tales, reserving myself to complete the rest at a more convenient season and at greater leisure.

However, as men are fond of novelties, I was solicited with very pressing requests to pursue my point, to which I consented, rather by reason of the importunity than of my own will, and my enterprise was conducted in such fashion, that so as not to show myself in any wise disobedient, I added some more tales, to which again others have since been adjoined.

In regard to myself, I can assure thee that it would have been less difficult for me to build the whole edifice anew than to mutilate it in several places, change, innovate, add and suppress in others, but I was almost perforce compelled to give it a new form, which I have done, partly for the requirements and the adornment of the stories, partly to conform to the times and the infelicity of our century, when most human things are so exulcerated that there is no work, however well digested, polished, and filed, but it is badly interpreted and slandered by the malice of fastidious persons. Take, therefore, in good part our hasty labor, and be not too close a censor of another's work until thou hast examined thine own.

---

* This notice follows the dedicatory preface in the edition of 1558.

To the most Illustrious and
Virtuous Princess
Madame Jane de Foix
Queen of Navarre

*C*laud Gruget, her very humble servant, presents salutation and wishes of felicity.*

I would not have interfered, Madam, to present you with this book of the Tales of the late Queen, your mother, if the first edition had not omitted or concealed her name, and almost entirely changed its form, to such a point that many did not recognize it; on which account, to render it worthy of its author, I, as soon as it was divulged, gathered together from all sides the copies I could collect of it written by hand, verifying them by my copy, and acting in such wise that I arranged the book in the real order in which she had drawn it up. Then, with the permission of the King and your consent, it was sent to the press to be published such as it should be.

Concerning it, I am reminded of what Count Balthazar says of Boccaccio in the Preface to his *Courtier*† that what he had done by way of pastime, namely, his *Decameron,* had brought him more honor than all his other works in Latin or Tuscan, which he esteemed the most serious.

Thus, the Queen, that true ornament of our century, from whom you do not derogate in the love and knowledge of good letters, while amusing herself with the acts of human life, has left such beauteous instructions that there is no one who does not find matter of erudition

---

* This preface was inserted in the edition issued in 1559 by Claud Gruget, who gave the title of *"Heptameron"* to Queen Margaret's tales.

† The *Libro del Cortegiano,* by Count Baldassare Castiglione, was the nobleman's *vade-mecum* of the period. First published at Venice in 1528, it was translated into French in 1537 by J. Colin, secretary to Francis I — Ed.

in them; and, indeed, according to all good judgment, she has surpassed Boccaccio in the beautiful Discourses which she composes upon each of her tales. For which she deserves praise, not only over the most excellent ladies, but also among the most learned men; for of the three styles of oration described by Cicero, she has chosen the simple one, similar to that of Terence in Latin, which to everyone seems very easy to imitate, though it is anything but that to him who tries it.

It is true that such a present will not be new to you, and that you will only recognize in it the maternal inheritance. However, I feel assured that you will receive it favorably, at seeing it, in this second impression, restored to its original state, for according to what I have heard the first displeased you. Not that he who put his hand to it was not a learned man, or did not take trouble; indeed it is easy to believe that he was not minded to disguise it thus, without some reason; nevertheless his work has proved unpleasing.

I present it to you then, Madam, not that I pretend to any share in it, but only as having unmasked it to restore it to you in its natural state. It is for Your Royal Greatness to favor it since it proceeds from your illustrious House, whereof it bears the mark upon the front, which will serve it as a safe-conduct throughout the world and render it welcome among good company.

As for myself, recognizing the honor that you will do me in receiving from my hand the work thus restored to its right state, I shall ever feel obliged to render you most humble duty.

Prologue

On the first day of September, when the baths in the Pyrenees Mountains begin to be possessed of their virtue, there were at those of Cauterets* many persons as well of France as of Spain, some to drink the water, others to bathe in it, and again others to make trial of the mud; all these being remedies so marvelous that persons despaired of by the doctors return thence wholly cured. My purpose is not to speak to you of the situation or virtue of the said baths, but only to set forth as much as relates to the matter of which I desire to write.

All the sick persons continued at the baths for more than three weeks, until by the amendment in their condition they perceived that they might return home again. But while they were preparing to do so, there fell such extraordinary rains that it seemed as though God had forgotten the promise He made to Noah never to destroy the world with water again; for every cottage and every lodging in Cauterets was so flooded with water that it was no longer possible to continue there. Those who had come from the side of Spain returned thither across the mountains as best they could, and such of them as knew whither the roads led fared best in making their escape.

The French lords and ladies thought to return to Tarbes as easily as they had come, but they found the streamlets so deep as to be scarcely fordable. When they came to pass over the Bearnese Gave,† which at

---

* There are no fewer than twenty-six sources at Cauterets, the waters being either of a sulfurous or a saline character. The mud baths alluded to by Margaret were formerly taken at the Source de César Vieux, halfway up Mount Peyraute, and so called owing to a tradition that Julius Cæsar bathed there. It is at least certain that these baths were known to the Romans. – Ed.

Cauterets is frequently mentioned by the old authors, and Rabelais refers to it in this passage: "Pantagruel's urine was so hot that ever since that time it has not cooled, and you have some of it in France, at divers places, at Coderetz, Limous, Dast, Ballerue, Bourbonne, and elsewhere"(Book ii. chap, xxxiii.). – M.

† The Basques give the name of Gave to those watercourses which become torrents in certain seasons. The Bearnese Gave, so named because it passes through the

the time of their former passage had been less than two feet in depth, they found it so broad and swift that they turned aside to seek for the bridges. But these being only of wood, had been swept away by the turbulence of the water.

Then certain of the company thought to stem the force of the current by crossing in a body, but they were quickly carried away, and the others who had been about to follow lost all inclination to do so. Accordingly they separated, as much because they were not all of one mind as to find some other way. Some crossed over the mountains, and passing through Aragon came to the county of Rousillon, and thence to Narbonne; whilst others made straight for Barcelona, going thence by sea, some to Marseilles and others to Aigues-Mortes.

But a widow lady of long experience, named Oisille, resolved to lay aside all fear of bad roads and to betake herself to Our Lady of Serrance.*

She was not, indeed, so superstitious as to think that the glorious Virgin would leave her seat at her Son's right hand to come and dwell in a desolate country, but she was desirous to see the hallowed spot of which she had so often heard, and further she was sure that if there were a means of escaping from a danger, the monks would certainly find it out. At last she arrived, after passing through places so strange, and so difficult in the going up and coming down, that, in spite of her years and weight, she had perforce gone most of the way on foot But the most piteous thing was, that the greater part of her servants and horses were left dead on the way, and she had but one man and one woman with her on arriving at Serrance, where she was charitably received by the monks.

There were also among the French two gentlemen who had gone to the baths rather that they might be in the company of the ladies whose lovers they were, than because of any failure in their health. These

---

territory of the ancient city of Beam, takes its source in the Pyrenees, and flows past Pau to Sorde, where it joins the Adour, which falls into the sea at Bayonne. It is nowadays generally known as the Gave of Pau. — L. & M.

* The Abbey of Our Lady of Serrance, or more correctly Sarrances, in the valley of Aspe, was occupied by monks of the Prémontré Order, who were under the patronage of St. Mary. An apparition of the Virgin having been reported in the vicinity, pilgrimages were made to Sarrances on the feasts of her nativity (Sept. 8) and her assumption (Aug. 15). In 1385 Gaston de Foix, who greatly enriched the abbey, built a residence in the neighborhood, his example being followed by the Gramonts, the Miollens, and other nobles. The pilgrimages had become very celebrated in the fifteenth century, when Louis XI repaired to Sarrances, accompanied by Coictier, his physician. In 1569, however, the Huguenots pillaged and burned down the abbey, together with the royal and other residences. The monks who escaped the flames were put to the sword. — M. & Ed.

gentlemen, seeing that the company was departing and that the husbands of their ladies were taking them away, resolved to follow them at
a distance without making their design known to anyone. But one
evening, while the two married gentlemen and their wives were in the
house of one who was more of a robber than a peasant, the two lovers,
who were lodged in a farmhouse hard by, heard about midnight a great
uproar. They got up, together with their serving-men, and inquired what
this tumult meant. The poor man, in great fear, told them that it was
caused by certain evil-doers who were come to share the spoil which was
in the house of their fellow-bandit. Thereupon the gentlemen immediately took their arms, and with their serving-men set forth to succor the
ladies, esteeming it a happier thing to die for them than to outlive them.

When they reached the house, they found the first door broken
through, and the two gentlemen with their servants defending themselves valiantly. But inasmuch as they were outnumbered by the robbers,
and were also sorely wounded, they were beginning to fall back, having
already lost many of their servants. The two gentlemen, looking in at
the windows, perceived the ladies shrieking and sobbing so bitterly that
their hearts swelled with pity and love at the sight; and, like two enraged
bears coming down from the mountains, they fell upon the bandits with
such fury that many of them were slain, while the remainder, unwilling
to await their onset, fled to a hiding place which was known to them.

When the gentlemen had worsted these rogues and had slain the host
himself among the rest, they heard that the man's wife was even worse
than her husband; and they therefore sent her after him with a sword-
thrust. Then they entered a lower room, where they found one of the
married gentlemen on the point of death. The other had received no
hurt, save that his clothes were all pierced with thrusts and that his sword
was broken in two. The poor gentleman, perceiving what help the two
had afforded him, embraced and thanked them, and besought them not
to abandon him, which was to them a very agreeable request. When they
had buried the dead gentleman, and had comforted his wife as well as
they were able, they took the road which God set before them, not
knowing whither they were going.

If it pleases you to know the names of the three gentlemen, the
married one was called Hircan, and his wife Parlamente, the name of
the widow being Longarine; of the two lovers one was called Dagoucin
and the other Saffredent. After having been the whole day on horseback,
towards evening they descried a belfry, whither with toil and trouble
they made the best of their way, and on their arrival were kindly received
by the Abbot and the monks. The abbey is called St. Savyn.*

The Abbot, who came of an ancient line, lodged them honorably, and when taking them to their apartments inquired of them concerning their adventures. When he had heard the truth, he told them that others had fared as badly as they, for in one of his rooms he had two ladies who had escaped a like danger, or perchance a greater, inasmuch as they had had to do with beasts, and not with men.* Half a league on this side of Peyrechitte† the poor ladies had met with a bear coming down from the mountain, before whom they had fled with such speed that

---

* The Abbey of St. Savin of Tarbes, situated between Argelèz and Pierrefitte, in what was formerly called the county of Lavedan, is stated to have been founded by Charlemagne; and here the Paladin Roland is said to have slain the giants Alabaster and Passamont to recompense the monks for their hospitality. The abbey took its name from a child (the son of a Count of Barcelona) who led a hermit's life, and is accredited with having performed several miracles in the neighborhood. About the year 1100 the Pope, siding with the people of the valley of Aspe in a quarrel between them and the Abbot of St. Savin, issued a bull forbidding the women of Lavedan to conceive for a period of seven years. The animals, moreover, were not to bring forth young, and the trees were not to bear fruit for a like period. The edict remained in force for six years, when the Abbot of St. Savin compromised matters by engaging to pay an annual tribute to Aspe. This tribute was actually paid until the Revolution of 1789. On the other hand, the abbey was entitled to the right shoulder of every stag, boar, and izard (the Pyrenean chamois) killed in the valley, with other tributes of trout, cheese, and flowers, which last the Abbot acknowledged by kissing the prettiest maiden of Argelèz. Amongst various privileges possessed by the monks was that of having their beds made by the girls of the neighborhood on certain high days and holidays.

In the tenth century Raymond of Bigorre presented the abbey with the valley of Cauterets on condition that a church should be built there and "sufficient houses kept in repair to facilitate the using of the baths." In 1290 Edward III of England confirmed the monks of St. Savin in possession of Cauterets. In 1316, when the inhabitants of the latter place wished to change the situation of their village, the Abbot of St. Savin consented, but a woman opposed her veto (all women had the right of vote) and this sufficed to frustrate the scheme. The abbey derived a considerable income from Cauterets, the baths and the houses built there for the accommodation of visitors being let out on lease. The leases of 1617 and 1697 are preserved in the archives of Pau. In the time of Queen Margaret the abbey was extremely wealthy; the Abbot to whom she refers, according to M. Le Roux de Lincy, was probably Raymond de Fontaine, who ruled St. Savin from 1534 to 1540, under the authority of the commendatory abbots, Anthony de Rochefort and Nicholas Dangu, Bishop of Séez. Some of the commentators of the *Heptameron* believe the latter to have been the original "Dagoucin" who is supposed to tell several of the tales. — Ed.

* In two MS. copies of the *Heptameron* in the Bibliothèque Nationale, Paris, numbered respectively 1520 and 1524, after the words "not with men" there follows "in men there is some mercy, but in animals none." — L.

† Peyrechitte is evidently intended for Pierrefitte, a village on the left bank of the Gave, between Argelèz and Cauterets. — Ed.

their horses fell dead under them at the abbey gates. Further, two of their women who arrived a long time afterwards had made report that the bear had killed all the serving-men.

Then the two ladies and the three gentlemen entered the room where these unhappy travelers were, and found them weeping. They recognized them to be Nomerfide and Ennasuite, whereupon they all embraced and recounted what had befallen them. At the exhortations of the good Abbot they began to take comfort in having found one another again, and in the morning they heard mass with much devotion, praising God for the perils from which they had escaped.

While they were all at mass there came into the church* a man clad only in a shirt, fleeing as though he were pursued, and crying out for aid. Forthwith Hircan and the other gentlemen went to meet him to see what the affair might mean, and perceived two men behind him with drawn swords.

These, on seeing so great a company, sought to fly, but they were hotly pursued by Hircan and his companions, and so lost their lives. When Hircan came back, he found that the man in the shirt was one of his companions named Geburon, who related to them how while he was in bed at a farmhouse near Peyrechitte three men came upstairs, and how he, although he was in his shirt and had no other weapon but his sword, had stretched one of them on the ground mortally wounded. While the other two were occupied in raising their companion, he, perceiving himself to be naked and the others armed, bethought him that he could not outdo them except it were by flight, as being the least encumbered with clothes. And so he had escaped, and for this he praised God and those who had avenged him.

When they had heard mass and had dined they sent to see if it was possible to cross the river Gave, and on learning that it was not, they were in great dismay. However, the Abbot urgently entreated them to stay with him until the water had abated, and they agreed to remain for that day.

In the evening, as they were going to bed, there arrived an aged monk who was wont to come in September of every year to Our Lady of Serrance. They inquired of him concerning his journey, and he told them that on account of the floods he had come over the mountains

---

* This church is still in existence. It is mainly in the Romanesque style and almost destitute of ornamentation. There are, however, some antique paintings of St. Savin's miracles; and the saint's tomb, which is still preserved, is considered to be some twelve hundred years old. The village is gathered about the church, and forms a wide street lined with houses of the fifteenth century, which Margaret and her friends must have gazed upon during their sojourn here. — Ed.

and by the worst roads he had ever known. On the way he had seen a very pitiful sight. He had met a gentleman named Simontault, who, wearied by his long waiting for the river to subside, and trusting to the goodness of his horse, had tried to force a passage, and had placed all his servants round about him to break the force of the current. But when they were in the midst of the stream, those who were the worst mounted were swept away, horses and men, down the stream, and were never seen again. The gentleman, finding himself alone, turned his horse to go back, but before he could reach the bank his horse sank under him. Nevertheless, God willed that this should happen so close to the bank that the gentleman was able, by dragging himself on all fours and not without swallowing a great deal of water, to scramble out on to the hard stones, though he was then so weak and weary that he could not stand upright.

By good fortune a shepherd, bringing back his sheep at even, found him seated among the stones, wet to the skin, and sad not only for himself but on account of his servants whom he had seen perish before his eyes. The shepherd, who understood his need even better from his appearance than from his speech, took him by the hand and led him to his humble dwelling, where he kindled some faggots, and so dried him in the best way that he could. The same evening God led thither this good monk, who showed him the road to Our Lady of Serrance assuring him that he would be better lodged there than anywhere else, and would there find an aged widow named Oisille who had been as unfortunate as himself.

When all the company heard tell of the good Lady Oisille and the gentle knight Simontault, they were exceedingly glad, and praised the Creator, who, content with the sacrifice of serving-folk, had preserved their masters and mistresses. And more than all the rest did Parlamente give hearty praise to God, for Simontault had long been her devoted lover.

Then they made diligent inquiry concerning the road to Serrance, and although the good old man declared it to be very difficult, they were not to be debarred from attempting to proceed thither that very day. They set forth well furnished with all that was needful, for the Abbot provided them with wine and abundant victuals,* and with willing companions to lead them safely over the mountains.

---

* According to MS. No. 1520 (Bib. Nat., Paris), the Abbot also furnished them with the best horses of Lavedan and good "cappes" of Beam. The Lavedan horses were renowned for their speed and spirit, and the Bearnese cappe was a cloak provided with a hood. — B. J.

These they crossed more often on foot than on horseback, and after much toil and sweat came to Our Lady of Serrance. Here the Abbot, although somewhat evilly disposed, durst not deny them lodging for fear of the Lord of Beam,* who, as he was aware, held them in high esteem. Being a true hypocrite, he showed them as fair a countenance as he could, and took them to see the Lady Oisille and the gentle knight Simontault.

The joyfulness of all this company who had been thus miraculously brought together was so great that the night seemed short to them while praising God in the Church for the goodness that He had shown to them. When towards morning they had taken a little rest, they all went to hear mass and receive the holy sacrament of fellowship, in which all Christians are joined together as one, imploring Him who of His mercy had thus united them, that He would further their journey to His glory. After they had dined they sent to learn whether the waters were at all abated, and found that, on the contrary, they were rather increased, and could not be crossed with safety for a long time to come. They therefore determined to make a bridge resting on two rocks which come very close together, and where there are still planks for those foot-passengers who, coming from Oleron, wish to avoid crossing at the ford. The Abbot was well pleased that they should make this outlay, to the end that the number of pilgrims might be increased, and he furnished them with workmen, though he was too avaricious to give them a single farthing.

The workmen declared that they could not finish the bridge in less than ten or twelve days, and all the company, both ladies and gentlemen, began to grow weary. But Parlamente, who was Hircan's wife, and who was never idle or melancholy, asked leave of her husband to speak, and said to the aged Lady Oisille —

"I am surprised, madam, that you who have so much experience, and now fill the place of mother to all of us women, do not devise some pastime to relieve the weariness we shall feel during our long stay; for if we have not some pleasant and virtuous occupation we shall be in danger of falling ill."

"Nay," added the young widow Longarine, "worse than that, we shall become ill-tempered, which is an incurable disease; for there is not one among us but has cause to be exceeding downcast, having regard to our several losses."

Ennasuite laughing replied —

---

* The Kings of Navarre had been Lords of Beam for two centuries, but Beam still retained its old customs and had its special government. The Lord of Beam here referred to was Henry d'Albret, Margaret's second husband. — B. J.

"Everyone has not lost her husband like you, and the loss of servants need not bring despair, since others may readily be found. Nevertheless, I too am of opinion that we should have some pleasant exercise with which to while away the time, for otherwise we shall be dead by tomorrow."

All the gentlemen agreed with what these ladies said, and begged Oisille to tell them what they should do.

"My children," she replied, "you ask me for something which I find very difficult to teach you, namely, a pastime that may deliver you from your weariness. I have sought for such a remedy all my life and have never found but one, which is the reading of the Holy Scriptures. In them the mind may find that true and perfect joy from which repose and bodily health proceed. If you would know by what means I continue so blithe and healthy in my old age, it is because on rising I immediately take up the Holy Scriptures* and read therein, and so perceive and contemplate the goodness of God, who sent His Son into the world to proclaim to us the Sacred Word and glad tidings by which He promises the remission of all sins and the satisfaction of all debts by the gift that He has made us of His love, passion, and merits.

"The thought of this gives me such joy that I take my Psalter and in all humility sing with my heart and utter with my lips the sweet psalms and canticles which the Holy Spirit put into the heart of David and of other writers. And so acceptable is the contentment that this brings to me, that any evils which may befall me during the day I look upon as blessings, seeing that I have in my heart, through faith, Him who has borne them all for me. In the same way before supper I retire to feed my soul by reading, and then in the evening I call to mind all I have done during the past day, in order that I may ask forgiveness for my sins, thank Him for His mercies, and, feeling safe from all harm, take my rest in His love, fear, and peace. This, my children, is the pastime I have long practiced, after making trial of all others and finding in none contentment of spirit. I believe that if you give an hour every morning to reading and then offer up devout prayers during mass, you will find in this lonely place all the beauty that any town could afford. One who knows God sees all things fair in Him, and without Him everything seems uncomely; wherefore, I pray you, accept my advice, if you would live in gladness."

Then Hircan took up the discourse and said —

---

* Margaret read a portion of the Scriptures every day, saying that the perusal preserved one "from all sorts of evils and diabolical temptations" (*Histoire de Foix, Béarn, et Navarre,* by P. Olhagaray, Paris, 1609, p. 502). — L.

"Those, madam, who have read the Holy Scriptures, as I believe we all have done, will acknowledge that what you have said is true. You must, however, consider that we are not yet so mortified that we have not need of some pastime and bodily exercise. When we are at home we have the chase and hawking, which cause us to lay aside a thousand foolish thoughts, and the ladies have their household cares, their work, and sometimes the dance, in all which they find honorable exercise. So, speaking on behalf of the men, I propose that you, who are the oldest, read to us in the morning about the life that was led by Our Lord Jesus Christ and the great and wonderful works that He did for us; and that between dinner and vespers we choose some pastime that shall be pleasant to the body and yet not hurtful to the soul. In this way we shall pass the day cheerfully."

The Lady Oisille replied that she had been at pains to forget every description of worldly vanity, and she therefore feared that she should succeed but ill in the choice of such an entertainment. The matter must be decided by the majority of opinions, and she begged Hircan to set forth his own first.

"For my part," said he, "if I thought that the pastime I should choose would be as agreeable to the company as to myself, my opinion would soon be given. For the present, however, I withhold it, and will abide by what the rest shall say."

His wife Parlamente, thinking he referred to her, began to blush, and, half in anger and half laughing, replied —

"Perhaps, Hircan, she who you think would find it most dull might readily find means of compensation had she a mind for it. But let us leave aside a pastime in which only two can share, and speak of one that shall be common to all."

"Since my wife has understood the meaning of my words so well," said Hircan to all the ladies, "and a private pastime is not to her liking, I think she will be better able than anyone else to name one that all may enjoy; and I herewith give in to her opinion, having no other of my own."

To this all the company agreed.

Parlamente, perceiving that it had fallen to her to decide, spoke as follows —

"Did I find myself as capable as the ancients who invented the arts, I should devise some sport or pastime in fulfillment of the charge you lay upon me. But knowing as I do my knowledge and capacity, which are scarcely able to recall the worthy performances of others, I shall think myself happy if I can follow closely such as have already satisfied your request. Among the rest, I think there is not one of you who has not

read the Hundred Tales of Boccaccio,$FMargaret here alludes to the
French translation of the *Decameron* made by her secretary, Anthony le
Maçon, and first issued in Paris in 1545. Messrs. De Lincy and Montaiglon accordingly think that the prologue of the *Heptameron* was
written subsequently to that date; but M. Dillaye states that Le Maçon's
translation was circulated at Court in manuscript long before it was
printed. This contention is in some measure borne out by Le Maçon's
dedication to Margaret, of which the more interesting passages are given
in the Appendix to this volume (A). — ED. lately translated from the
Italian into French. So highly were these thought of by King Francis,
first of that name, Monseigneur the Dauphin,* Madame the Dauphiness, and Madame Margaret, that could Boccaccio have only heard them
from the place where he lay, the praise of such illustrious persons would
have raised him from the dead.

Now I heard not long since that the two ladies I have mentioned,
together with several others of the Court, determined to do like Boccaccio, with, however, one exception — they would not write any story
that was not a true one. And the said ladies, and Monseigneur the
Dauphin with them, undertook to tell ten stories each, and to assemble
in all ten persons, from among those whom they thought the most
capable of relating something. Such as had studied and were people of
letters were excepted, for Monseigneur the Dauphin would not allow of
their art being brought in, fearing lest the flowers of rhetoric should in
some wise prove injurious to the truth of the tales. But the weighty
affairs in which the King had engaged, the peace between him and the
King of England, the bringing to bed of the Dauphiness,† and many
other matters of a nature to engross the whole Court, caused the
enterprise to be entirely forgotten.

---

* The Dauphin here mentioned is Francis I's second son, who subsequently reigned
  as Henry II. He became Dauphin by the death of his elder brother on August 10,
  1536. The Dauphiness is Catherine de' Medici, the wife of Henry, whom he married
  in 1533; whilst Madame Margaret, according to M. de Montaiglon, is the Queen
  of Navarre herself, she being usually called by that name at her brother's Court. M.
  Dillaye, who is of a different opinion, maintains that the Queen would not write
  so eulogistically of herself, and that she evidently refers to her brother's daughter,
  Margaret de Berry, born in 1523, and married to the Duke of Savoy. — Ed.

† The confinement mentioned here is that of Catherine de Medici, who, after
  remaining childless during ten years of wedlock, gave birth to a son, afterwards
  Francis II, in January 1543. The peace previously spoken of would appear to be that
  signed at Crespy in September 1544. Both M. de Montaiglon and M. Dillaye are of
  opinion, however, that a word or two is deficient in the MS., and that Margaret
  intended to imply the rupture of peace in 1543, when Henry VIII allied himself
  with the Emperor Charles V against Francis I — Ed.

By reason, however, of our now great leisure, it can be accomplished in ten days, whilst we wait for our bridge to be finished. If it so pleased you, we might go every day from noon till four of the clock into yonder pleasant meadow beside the river Gave. The trees there are so leafy that the sun can neither penetrate the shade nor change the coolness to heat. Sitting there at our ease, we might each one tell a story of something we have ourselves seen, or heard related by one worthy of belief. At the end of ten days we shall have completed the hundred,* and if God wills it that our work be found worthy in the eyes of the lords and ladies I have mentioned, we will on our return from this journey present them with it, in lieu of images and paternosters,† (15) and feeling assured that they will hold this to be a more pleasing gift. If, however, anyone can devise some plan more agreeable than mine, I will fall in with his opinion."

All the company replied that it was not possible to give better advice, and that they awaited the morning in impatience, in order to begin.

Thus they spent that day joyously, reminding one another of what they had seen in their time. As soon as the morning was come they went to the room of Madame Oisille, whom they found already at her prayers. They listened to her reading for a full hour, then piously heard mass, and afterwards went to dinner at ten o'clock.‡

After dinner each one withdrew to his chamber, and did what he had to do. According to their plan, at noon they failed not to return to the meadow, which was so fair and pleasant that it would need a Boccaccio to describe it as it really was; suffice to say that a fairer was never seen.

When the company were all seated on the green grass, which was so fine and soft that they needed neither cushion nor carpet, Simontault commenced by saying —

"Which of us shall begin before the others?"

"Since you were the first to speak," replied Hircan, "'tis reasonable that you should rule us; for in sport we are all equal."

"Would to God," said Simontault, "I had no worse fortune in this world than to be able to rule all the company present."

---

*   This passage plainly indicates that the Queen meant to pen a Decameron. — Ed.
†   This is an allusion to the holy images, medals, and chaplets which people brought back with them from pilgrimages. — B. J.
‡   At that period ten o'clock was the Court dinner-hour. Fifty years earlier people used to dine at eight in the morning. Louis XII, however, changed the hour of his meals to suit his wife, Mary of England, who had been accustomed to dine at noon. — B. J.

On hearing this Parlamente, who well knew what it meant, began to cough. Hircan, therefore, did not perceive the color that came into her cheeks, but told Simontault to begin, which he did as presently follows.

FIRST DAY

On the First Day are recounted the ill-turns which have been done by Women to Men and by Men to Women.

Tale I

The wife of a Proctor, having been pressingly solicited by the Bishop of Sees, took him for her profit, and, being as little satisfied with him as with her husband, found a means to have the son of the Lieutenant-General of Alençon for her pleasure. Some time afterwards she caused the latter to be miserably murdered by her husband, who, although he obtained pardon for the murder, was afterwards sent to the galleys with a sorcerer named Gallery; and all this was brought about by the wickedness of his wife.*

*L*adies, said Simontault, I have been so poorly rewarded for my long service, that to avenge myself upon Love, and upon her who treats me so cruelly, I shall be at pains to make a collection of all the ill turns that women hath done to hapless men; and moreover I will relate nothing but the simple truth.

In the town of Alençon, during the lifetime of Charles, the last Duke,† there was a Proctor named St. Aignan, who had married a gentlewoman of the neighborhood. She was more beautiful than virtuous, and on account of her beauty and light behavior was much sought after by the Bishop of Sees,‡ who, in order to compass his ends, managed

---

* The incidents of this story are historical, and occurred in Alençon and Paris between 1520 and 1525. — L.

† The Duke Charles here alluded to is Margaret's first husband. — Ed.

‡ Sees or Séez, on the Orne, thirteen miles from Alençon, and celebrated for its Gothic cathedral, is one of the oldest bishoprics in Normandy. Richard Coeur-de-Lion is said to have here done penance and obtained absolution for his conduct towards his father, Henry II. At the time of this story the Bishop of Sees was James de Silly, whose father, also James de Silly, Lord of Lonray, Vaux-Pacey, &c, a favorite and chamberlain of King Louis XII, became Master of the Artillery of France in 1501. The second James de Silly — born at Caen — was ordained Bishop of Sees on February 26th, 1511; he was also Abbot of St. Vigor and St. Pierre-sur-Dives, where he restored and beautified the abbatial church. In 1519 he consecrated a convent for women of noble birth, founded by Margaret and her first husband at Essey, twenty miles from Alençon, the ruins of which still exist. A year later Francis Rometens dedicated to him an edition of the letters of Pico della Mirandola. He died April 24th, 1539,

the husband so well, that the latter not only failed to perceive the vicious conduct of his wife and of the Bishop, but was further led to forget the affection he had always shown in the service of his master and mistress.

Thus, from being a loyal servant, he became utterly adverse to them, and at last sought out sorcerers to procure the death of the Duchess.* Now for a long time the Bishop consorted with this unhappy woman, who submitted to him from avarice rather than from love, and also because her husband urged her to show him favor. But there was a youth in the town of Alençon, son of the Lieutenant-General,† whom she loved so much that she was half crazy regarding him; and she often availed herself of the Bishop to have some commission entrusted to her husband, so that she might see the son of the Lieutenant, who was named Du Mesnil, at her ease.

This mode of life lasted a long time, during which she had the Bishop for her profit and the said Du Mesnil for her pleasure. To the latter she swore that she showed a fair countenance to the Bishop only that their own love might the more freely continue; that the Bishop, in spite of appearances, had obtained only words, from her; and that he, Du Mesnil, might rest assured that no man, save himself, should ever receive aught else.

One day, when her husband was setting forth to visit the Bishop, she asked leave of him to go into the country, saying that the air of the town was injurious to her; and, when she had arrived at her farm, she forthwith wrote to Du Mesnil to come and see her, without fail, at about ten o'clock in the evening. This the young man did; but as he was entering at the gate he met the maid who was wont to let him in, and who said to him, "Go elsewhere, friend, for your place is taken."

Supposing that the husband had arrived, he asked her how matters stood. The woman, seeing that he was so handsome, youthful, and well-bred, and was withal so loving and yet so little loved, took pity upon him and told him of his mistress's wantonness, thinking that on hearing this he would be cured of loving her so much. She related to him that the Bishop of Sees had but just arrived, and was now in bed with the lady, a thing which the latter had not expected, for he was not to have come until the morrow. However, he had detained her husband

---

at Fleury-sur-Aiidellé, about fifteen miles from Rouen, and was buried in his episcopal church. (See *Gallia Christiana,* vol. xi. p. 702.) His successor in the See of Sees was Nicholas Danguye, or Dangu (a natural son of Cardinal Duprat), with whom M. Frank tries to identify Dagoucin, one of the narrators of the *Heptameron.* — L. and Ed.

* This was of course Margaret herself. — Ed

† Gilles du Mesnil, Lieutenant-General of the presidial bailiwick and Sénéchaussée of Alençon. — B. J.

at his house, and had stolen away at night to come secretly and see her. If ever man was in despair it was Du Mesnil, who nevertheless was quite unable to believe the story. He hid himself, however, in a house near by, and watched until three hours after midnight, when he saw the Bishop come forth disguised, yet not so completely but that he could recognize him more readily than he desired.

Du Mesnil in his despair returned to Alençon, whither, likewise, his wicked mistress soon came, and went to speak to him, thinking to deceive him according to her wont. But he told her that, having touched sacred things, she was too holy to speak to a sinner like himself, albeit his repentance was so great that he hoped his sin would very soon be forgiven him. When she learnt that her deceit was found out, and that excuses, oaths, and promises never to act in a like way again were of no avail, she complained of it to her Bishop. Then, having weighed the matter with him, she went to her husband and told him that she could no longer dwell in the town of Alençon, for the Lieutenant's son, whom he had so greatly esteemed among his friends, pursued her unceasingly to rob her of her honor. She therefore begged of him to abide at Argentan,* in order that all suspicion might be removed.

The husband, who suffered himself to be ruled by his wife, consented; but they had not been long at Argentan when this bad woman sent a message to Du Mesnil, saying that he was the wickedest man in the world, for she knew full well that he had spoken evilly (sic.) of her and of the Bishop of Sees; however, she would strive her best to make him repent of it.

The young man, who had never spoken of the matter except to herself, and who feared to fall into the bad graces of the Bishop, repaired to Argentan with two of his servants, and finding his mistress at vespers in the church of the Jacobins,† he went and knelt beside her, and said —

"I am come hither, madam, to swear to you before God that I have never spoken of your honor to any person but yourself. You treated me so ill that I did not make you half the reproaches you deserved; but if there be man or woman ready to say that I have ever spoken of the matter to them, I am here to give them the lie in your presence."

Seeing that there were many people in the church, and that he was accompanied by two stout serving-men, she forced herself to speak as graciously as she could. She told him that she had no doubt he spoke the truth, and that she deemed him too honorable a man to make evil

---

* Argentan, on the Orne, twenty-six miles from Alençon, had been a distinct vis-county, but at this period it belonged to the duchy of Alençon. — Ed.

† The name of Jacobins was given to the monks of the Dominican Order, some of whom had a monastery in the suburbs of Argentan. — Ed.

report of anyone in the world; least of all of herself, who bore him so much friendship; but since her husband had heard the matter spoken of, she begged him to say in his presence that he had not so spoken and did not so believe.

To this he willingly agreed, and, wishing to attend her to her house, he offered to take her arm; but she told him it was not desirable that he should come with her, for her husband would think that she had put these words into his mouth. Then, taking one of his serving-men by the sleeve, she said —

"Leave me this man, and as soon as it is time I will send him to seek you. Meanwhile do you go and rest in your lodging."

He, having no suspicion of her conspiracy against him, went thither.

She gave supper to the serving-man whom she had kept with her, and who frequently asked her when it would be time to go and seek his master; but she always replied that his master would come soon enough. When it was night, she sent one of her own serving-men to fetch Du Mesnil; and he, having no suspicion of the mischief that was being prepared for him, went boldly to St. Aignan's house. As his mistress was still entertaining his servant there, he had but one with himself.

Just as he was entering the house, the servant who had been sent to him told him that the lady wished to speak with him before he saw her husband, and that she was waiting for him in a room where she was alone with his own serving-man; he would therefore do well to send his other servant away by the front door. This he did. Then while he was going up a small, dark stairway, the Proctor St. Aignan, who had placed some men in ambush in a closet, heard the noise, and demanded what it was; whereupon he was told that a man was trying to enter secretly into his house.

At the moment, a certain Thomas Guérin, a murderer by trade, who had been hired by the Proctor for the purpose, came forward and gave the poor young man so many sword-thrusts that whatever defense he was able to make could not save him from falling dead in their midst.

Meanwhile the servant who was waiting with the lady, said to her —

"I hear my master speaking on the stairway. I will go to him."

But the lady stopped him and said —

"Do not trouble yourself; he will come soon enough."

A little while afterwards the servant, hearing his master say, "I am dying, may God receive my soul!" wished to go to his assistance, but the lady again withheld him, saying —

"Do not trouble yourself; my husband is only chastising him for his follies. We will go and see what it is."

Then, leaning over the balustrade at the top of the stairway, she asked her husband —

"Well, is it done?"

"Come and see," he replied. "I have now avenged you on the man who put you to such shame."

So saying, he drove a dagger that he was holding ten or twelve times into the belly of a man whom, alive, he would not have dared to assail.

When the murder had been accomplished, and the two servants of the dead man had fled to carry the tidings to the unhappy father, St. Aignan bethought himself that the matter could not be kept secret. But he reflected that the testimony of the dead man's servants would not be believed, and that no one in his house had seen the deed done, except the murderers, and an old woman-servant, and a girl fifteen years of age. He secretly tried to seize the old woman, but, finding means to escape out of his hands, she sought sanctuary with the Jacobins,* and was afterwards the most trustworthy witness of the murder. The young maid remained for a few days in St. Aignan's house, but he found means to have her led astray by one of the murderers, and had her conveyed to a brothel in Paris so that her testimony might not be received.†

To conceal the murder, he caused the corpse of the hapless dead man to be burned, and the bones which were not consumed by the fire he caused to be placed in some mortar in a part of his house where he was building. Then he sent in all haste to the Court to sue for pardon, setting forth that he had several times forbidden his house to a person whom he suspected of plotting his wife's dishonor, and who, notwithstanding his prohibition, had come by night to see her in a suspicious fashion; whereupon, finding him in the act of entering her room, his anger had got the better of his reason and he had killed him.

But before he was able to dispatch his letter to the Chancellor's, the Duke and Duchess had been apprised by the unhappy father of the matter, and they sent a message to the Chancellor to prevent the granting of the pardon. Finding he could not obtain it, the wretched man fled to England with his wife and several of his relations. But before setting out he told the murderer who at his entreaty had done the deed, that he had seen expresses from the King directing that he should be taken

---

* It was still customary to take sanctuary in churches, monasteries, and convents at this date, although but little respect was shown for the refugees, whose hiding places were often surrounded so that they might be kept without food and forced to surrender. After being considerably restricted by an edict issued in 1515, the right of sanctuary was abolished by Francis I in 1539. — B. J. and D.

† Prostitutes were debarred from giving evidence in French courts of law at this period. — D.

and put to death. Nevertheless, on account of the service that he had rendered him, he desired to save his life, and he gave him ten crowns wherewith to leave the kingdom. The murderer did this, and was afterwards seen no more.

The murder was so fully proven by the servants of the dead man, by the woman who had taken refuge with the Jacobins, and by the bones that were found in the mortar, that legal proceedings were begun and completed in the absence of St. Aignan and his wife. They were judged by default and were both condemned to death. Their property was confiscated to the Prince, and fifteen hundred crowns were to be given to the dead man's father to pay the costs of the trial.

St. Aignan being in England and perceiving that in the eyes of the law he was dead in France, by means of his services to divers great lords and by the favor of his wife's relations, induced the King of England* to request the King of France† to grant him a pardon and restore him to his possessions and honors. But the King of France, having been informed of the wickedness and enormity of the crime, sent the process to the King of England, praying him to consider whether the offence was one deserving of pardon, and telling him that no one in the kingdom but the Duke of Alençon had the right to grant a pardon in that duchy. However, notwithstanding all his excuses, he failed to appease the King of England, who continued to entreat him so very pressingly that, at his request, the Proctor at last received a pardon and so returned to his own home.‡ There, to complete his wickedness, he consorted with a sorcerer named Gallery, hoping that by this man's art he might escape payment of the fifteen hundred crowns to the dead man's father.

To this end he went in disguise to Paris with his wife. She, finding that he used to shut himself up for a great while in a room with Gallery without acquainting her with the reason thereof, spied upon him one morning, and perceived Gallery showing him five wooden images, three of which had their hands hanging down, whilst two had them lifted up.[1]

---

* Henry VIII

† Francis I

‡ The letters of remission which were granted to St. Aignan on this occasion will be found in the Appendix to the First Day (B). It will be noted that Margaret in her story gives various particulars which St. Aignan did not fail to conceal in view of obtaining his pardon. — L.

[1] This refers to the superstitious practice called *envoûtement,* which, according to M. Léon de Laborde, was well known in France in 1316, and subsisted until the sixteenth century. In 1330 the famous Robert d'Artois, upon retiring to Brabant, occupied himself with pricking waxen images which represented King Philip VI, his brother-

"We must make waxen images like these," said Gallery, speaking to the Proctor. "Such as have their arms hanging down will be for those whom we shall cause to die, and the others with their arms raised will be for the persons from whom you would fain have love and favor."

"This one," said the Proctor, "shall be for the King by whom I would fain be loved, and this one for Monseigneur Brinon, Chancellor of Alençon."*

"The images," said Gallery, "must be set under the altar, to hear mass, with words that I will presently tell you to say."

Then, speaking of those images that had their arms lowered, the Proctor said that one should be for Master Gilles du Mesnil, father of the dead man, for he knew that as long as the father lived he would not cease to pursue him. Moreover, one of the women with their hands hanging down was to be for the Duchess of Alençon, sister to the King; for she bore so much love to her old servant, Du Mesnil, and had in so many other matters become acquainted with the Proctor's wickedness, that except she died he could not live. The second woman that had her arms hanging down was his own wife, who was the cause of all his misfortune, and who he felt sure would never amend her evil life.

When his wife, who could see everything through the keyhole, heard him placing her among the dead, she resolved to send him among them first. On pretence of going to borrow some money, she went to an uncle she had, named Neaufle, who was Master of Requests to the Duke of Alençon, and informed him of what she had seen and heard. Neaufle,

---

in-law, and the Queen, his sister. (*Mémoires de l'Académie des Inscriptions*, vol. xv. p. 426.) During the League the enemies of Henri III and the King of Navarre revived this practice. − (L.) It would appear also from a document in the Harley MSS. (18,452, Bib. N'at., Paris) that Cosmo Ruggieri, the Florentine astrologer, Catherine de' Medici's confidential adviser, was accused in 1574 of having made a wax figure in view of casting a spell upon Charles IX − M.

* John Brinon, Councilor of the King, President of the Parliament of Rouen, Chancellor of Alençon and Berry, Lord of Villaines (near Dreux), Remy, and Athueuil (near Montfort-l'Amaury), belonged to an old family of judicial functionaries. He was highly esteemed by Margaret, several of whose letters are addressed to him, and he was present at the signing of her marriage contract with Henry II of Navarre (Génin's *Lettres de Marguerite*, p. 444). He married Pernelle Perdrier, who brought him the lordship of Médan, near Poissy, and other important fiefs, which after his death she presented to the King. His praises were sung by Le Chandelier, the poet; and M. Floquet, in his History of the Parliament of Normandy, states that Brinon rendered most important services to France as a negotiator in Italy in 1521, and in England in 1524. The *Journal d'un Bourgeois de Paris* mentions that he died in Paris in 1528, aged forty-four, and was buried in the Church of St. Severin. − L. According to La Croix du Maine's *Bibliothèque Françoise*, Brinon was the author of a poem entitled *Les Amours de Sydire*. − B. J.

like the old and worthy servant that he was, went forthwith to the Chancellor of Alençon and told him the whole story.

As the Duke and Duchess of Alençon were not at Court that day, the Chancellor related this strange business to the Regent,* mother of the King and the Duchess, and she sent in all haste for the Provost of Paris,† who made such speed that he at once seized the Proctor and his sorcerer, Gallery. Without constraint or torture they freely confessed their guilt, and their case was made out and laid before the King.

Certain persons, wishing to save their lives, told him that they had only sought his good graces by their enchantments; but the King, holding his sister's life as dear as his own, commanded that the same sentence should be passed on them as if they had made an attempt on his own person.

However, his sister, the Duchess of Alençon, entreated that the Proctor's life might be spared, and the sentence of death be commuted to some heavy punishment. This request was granted her, and St. Aignan and Gallery were sent to the galleys of St. Blancart at Marseilles,‡ where they ended their days in close captivity, and had leisure to ponder on the grievousness of their crimes. The wicked wife, in the absence of her husband, continued in her sinful ways even more than before, and at last died in wretchedness.

"I pray you, ladies, consider what evil is caused by a wicked woman, and how many evils sprang from the sins of the one I have spoken of. You will find that ever since Eve caused Adam to sin, all women have set themselves to bring about the torment, slaughter and damnation of men. For myself, I have had such experience of their cruelty that I expect to die and be damned simply by reason of the despair into which one of them has cast me. And yet so great a fool am I, that I cannot but confess that hell coming from her hand is more pleasing than Paradise would be from the hand of another."

---

* Louise of Savoy.

† John de la Barre, a favorite of Francis I. See note to Tale lxiii. (vol. v.), in which he plays a conspicuous part. — Ed.

‡ This passage is explained by Henri Bouché, who states in his *Histoire Chronologique de Provençe* (vol. ii. p. 554), that after Francis I's voyage in captivity to Spain it was judged expedient that France should have several galleys in the Mediterranean, and that "orders were accordingly given for thirteen to be built at Marseilles — four for the Baron de Saint-Blancart, as many for Andrew Doria, &c." The Baron de Saint-Blancart here referred to was Bernard d'Ormezan, Admiral of the seas of the Levant, Conservator of the ports and tower of Aigues-Mortes, and General of the King's galleys. In 1523 he defeated the naval forces of the Emperor Charles V, and in 1525 conducted Margaret to Spain. — L. (See Memoir of Margaret, p. xli.)

Parlamente, pretending she did not understand that it was touching herself he spoke in this fashion, said to him —

"Since hell is as pleasant as you say, you ought not to fear the devil who has placed you in it."

"If my devil were to become as black as he has been cruel to me," answered Simontault angrily, "he would cause the present company as much fright as I find pleasure in looking upon them; but the fires of love make me forget those of this hell. However, to speak no further concerning this matter, I give my vote to Madame Oisille to tell the second story. I feel sure she would support my opinion if she were willing to say what she knows about women."

Forthwith all the company turned towards Oisille, and begged of her to proceed, to which she consented, and, laughing, began as follows —

"It seems to me, ladies, that he who has given me his vote has spoken so ill of our sex in his true story of a wicked woman, that I must call to mind all the years of my long life to find one whose virtue will suffice to gainsay his evil opinion. However, as I have bethought me of one worthy to be remembered, I will now relate her history to you."

Tale II

*The wife of a muleteer of Amboise chose rather to die cruelly at the hands of her servant than to fall in with his wicked purpose.**

*I*n the town of Amboise there was a muleteer in the service of the Queen of Navarre, sister to King Francis, first of that name. She being at Blois, where she had been brought to bed of a son, the aforesaid muleteer went thither to receive his quarterly payment, whilst his wife remained at Amboise in a lodging beyond the bridges.†

Now it happened that one of her husband's servants had long loved her exceedingly, and one day he could not refrain from speaking of it to her. She, however, being a truly virtuous woman, rebuked him so severely, threatening to have him beaten and dismissed by her husband, that from that time forth he did not venture to speak to her in any such way again or to let his love be seen, but kept the fire hidden within his breast until the day when his master had gone from home and his mistress was at vespers at St. Florentin,‡ the castle church, a long way from the muleteer's house.

Whilst he was alone the fancy took him that he might obtain by force what neither prayer nor service had availed to procure him, and accordingly he broke through a wooden partition which was between the chamber where his mistress slept and his own. The curtains of his

---

* The incidents of this story probably took place at Amboise, subsequent, however, to the month of August 1530, when Margaret was confined of her son John. — L.

† Amboise is on the left bank of the Loire, and there have never been any buildings on the opposite bank. However, the bridge over the river intersects the island of St. Jean, which is covered with houses, and here the muleteer's wife evidently resided. — M.

‡ The Church of St. Florentin here mentioned must not be confounded with that of the same name near one of the gates of Amboise. Erected in the tenth century by Foulques Nera of Anjou, it was a collegiate church, and was attended by the townsfolk, although it stood within the precincts of the château. For this reason Queen Margaret calls it the castle church. — Ed.

master's bed on the one side and of the servant's bed on the other so covered the walls as to hide the opening he had made; and thus his wickedness was not perceived until his mistress was in bed, together with a little girl eleven or twelve years old.

When the poor woman was in her first sleep, the servant, in his shirt and with his naked sword in his hand, came through the opening he had made in the wall into her bed; but as soon as she felt him beside her, she leaped out, addressing to him all such reproaches as a virtuous woman might utter. His love, however, was but bestial, and he would have better understood the language of his mules than her honorable reasonings; indeed, he showed himself even more bestial than the beasts with whom he had long consorted. Finding she ran so quickly round a table that he could not catch her, and that she was strong enough to break away from him twice, he despaired of ravishing her alive, and dealt her a terrible sword-thrust in the loins, thinking that, if fear and force had not brought her to yield, pain would assuredly do so.

The contrary, however, happened, for just as a good soldier, on seeing his own blood, is the more fired to take vengeance on his enemies and win renown, so her chaste heart gathered new strength as she ran fleeing from the hands of the miscreant, saying to him the while all she could think of to bring him to see his guilt. But so filled was he with rage that he paid no heed to her words. He dealt her several more thrusts, to avoid which she continued running as long as her legs could carry her.

When, after great loss of blood, she felt that death was near, she lifted her eyes to heaven, clasped her hands and gave thanks to God, calling Him her strength, her patience, and her virtue, and praying Him to accept her blood which had been shed for the keeping of His commandment and in reverence of His Son, through whom she firmly believed all her sins to be washed away and blotted out from the remembrance of His wrath.

As she was uttering the words, "Lord, receive the soul that has been redeemed by Thy goodness," she fell upon her face to the ground.

Then the miscreant dealt her several thrusts, and when she had lost both power of speech and strength of body, and was no longer able to make any defense, he ravished her.*

---

* Brantôme, in his account of Mary Queen of Scots, quotes this story. After mentioning that the headsman remained alone with the Queen's decapitated corpse, he adds: "He then took off her shoes and handled her as he pleased. It is suspected that he treated her in the same way as that miserable muleteer, in the Hundred Stories of the Queen of Navarre, treated the poor woman he killed. Stranger temptations than this come to men. After he (the executioner) had done as he chose, the (Queen's) body was carried into a room adjoining that of her servants." Lalanne's *Œuvres de Brantôme,* vol. vii. p. 438. — M.

Having thus satisfied his wicked lust, he fled in haste, and in spite of all pursuit was never seen again.

The little girl, who was in bed with the muleteer's wife, had hidden herself under the bed in her fear; but on seeing that the man was gone, she came to her mistress. Finding her to be without speech or movement, she called to the neighbors from the window for aid; and as they loved and esteemed her mistress as much as any woman that belonged to the town, they came forthwith, bringing surgeons with them. The latter found that she had received twenty-five mortal wounds in her body, and although they did what they could to help her, it was all in vain.

Nevertheless she lingered for an hour longer without speaking, yet making signs with eye and hand to show that she had not lost her understanding. Being asked by a priest in what faith she died, she answered, by signs as plain as any speech, that she placed her hope of salvation in Jesus Christ alone; and so with glad countenance and eyes upraised to heaven her chaste body yielded up its soul to its Creator.

Just as the corpse, having been laid out and shrouded,* was placed at the door to await the burial company, the poor husband arrived and beheld his wife's body in front of his house before he had even received tidings of her death. He inquired the cause of this, and found that he had double occasion to grieve; and his grief was indeed so great that it nearly killed him.

This martyr of chastity was buried in the Church of St. Florentin, and, as was their duty, all the upright women of Amboise failed not to show her every possible honor, deeming themselves fortunate in belonging to a town where so virtuous a woman had been found. And seeing the honor that was shown to the deceased, such women as were wanton and unchaste resolved to amend their lives.

"This, ladies, is a true story, which should incline us more strongly to preserve the fair virtue of chastity. We who are of gentle blood should die of shame on feeling in our hearts that worldly lust to avoid which the poor wife of a muleteer shrank not from so cruel a death. Some esteem themselves virtuous women who have never like this one resisted unto the shedding of blood. It is fitting that we should humble ourselves, for God does not vouchsafe His grace to men because of their birth or riches, but according as it pleases His own good-will. He pays no regard to persons, but chooses according to His purpose; and he whom He chooses He honors with all virtues. And often He chooses the lowly to confound those whom the world exalts and honors; for, as He Himself hath told us, 'Let us not rejoice in our merits, but rather

---

* Common people were then buried in shrouds, not in coffins. – Ed.

because our names are written in the Book of Life, from which nor death, nor hell, nor sin can blot them out.'"*

There was not a lady in the company but had tears of compassion in her eyes for the pitiful and glorious death of the muleteer's wife. Each thought within herself that, should fortune serve her in the same way, she would strive to imitate this poor woman in her martyrdom. Oisille, however, perceiving that time was being lost in praising the dead woman, said to Saffredent —

"Unless you can tell us something that will make the company laugh, I think none of them will forgive me for the fault I have committed in making them weep; wherefore I give you my vote for your telling of the third story."

Saffredent, who would gladly have recounted something agreeable to the company, and above all to one amongst the ladies, said that it was not for him to speak, seeing that there were others older and better instructed than himself, who should of right come first. Nevertheless, since the lot had fallen upon himself, he would rather have done with it at once, for the more numerous the good speakers before him, the worse would his own tale appear.

---

* These are not the exact words of Scripture, but a combination of several passages from the Book of Revelation. — Ed.

Tale III

The Queen of Naples, being wronged by King Alfonso, her husband, revenged herself with a gentleman whose wife was the King's mistress; and this intercourse lasted all their lives without the King at any time having suspicion of it.[*]

I have often desired, ladies, to be a sharer in the good fortune of the man whose story I am about to relate to you. You must know that in the time of King Alfonso,[†] whose lust was the scepter of his kingdom,[‡]

[*] This story is historical. The events occurred at Naples cir. 1450. — L.

[†] The King spoken of in this story must be Alfonso V, King of Aragon, who was born in 1385, and succeeded his father, Ferdinand the Just, in 1416. He had already made various expeditions to Sardinia and Corsica, when, in 1421, Jane II of Naples begged of him to assist her in her contest against Louis of Anjou. Alfonso set sail for Italy as requested, but speedily quarreled with Jane, on account of the manner in which he treated her lover, the Grand Seneschal Caraccioli. Jane, at her death in 1438, bequeathed her crown to René, brother of Louis of Anjou, whose claims Alfonso immediately opposed. Whilst blockading Gaëta he was defeated and captured, but ultimately set at liberty, whereupon he resumed the war. In 1442 he at last secured possession of Naples, and compelled René to withdraw from Italy. From that time Alfonso never returned to Spain, but settling himself in his Italian dominions, assumed the title of King of the Two Sicilies. He obtained the surname of the Magnanimous, from his generous conduct towards some conspirators, a list of whose names he tore to pieces unread, saying, "I will show these noblemen that I have more concern for their lives than they have themselves." The surname of the Learned was afterwards given to him from the circumstance that, like his rival René of Anjou, he personally cultivated letters, and also protected many of the leading learned men of Italy. Alfonso was fond of strolling about the streets of Naples unattended, and one day, when he was cautioned respecting this habit, he replied, "A father who walks abroad in the midst of his children has no cause for fear." Whilst possessed of many remarkable qualities, Alfonso, as Muratori and other writers have shown, was of an extremely licentious disposition. That he had no belief in conjugal fidelity is evidenced by his saying that "to ensure domestic happiness the husband should be deaf and the wife blind." He himself had several mistresses, and lived at variance with his wife, respecting whom some particulars are given in a note on page 69. He died in 1458, at the age of seventy-four,

there lived in the town of Naples a gentleman, so honorable, comely, and pleasant that his perfections induced an old gentleman to give him his daughter in marriage.

She vied with her husband in grace and comeliness, and there was great love between them, until a certain day in Carnival time, when the King went masked from house to house. All strove to give him the best welcome they could, but when he came to this gentleman's house he was entertained better than anywhere else, what with sweetmeats, and singers, and music, and, further, the fairest woman that, to his thinking, he had ever seen. At the end of the feast she sang a song with her husband in so graceful a fashion that she seemed more beautiful than ever.

The King, perceiving so many perfections united in one person, was not over pleased at the gentle harmony between the husband and wife, and deliberated how he might destroy it. The chief difficulty he met with was in the great affection which he observed existed between them, and on this account he hid his passion in his heart as deeply as he could. To relieve it in some measure, he gave many entertainments to the lords and ladies of Naples, and at these the gentleman and his wife were not forgotten. Now, inasmuch as men willingly believe what they desire, it seemed to the King that the glances of this lady gave him fair promise of future happiness, if only she were not restrained by her husband's presence. Accordingly, that he might learn whether his surmise was true, the King entrusted a commission to the husband, and sent him on a journey to Rome for a fortnight or three weeks.

As soon as the gentleman was gone, his wife, who had never before been separated from him, was in great distress; but the King comforted her as often as he was able, with gentle persuasions and presents, so that at last she was not only consoled, but well pleased with her husband's absence. Before the three weeks were over at the end of which he was to be home again, she had come to be so deeply in love with the King that her husband's return was no less displeasing to her than his departure had been. Not wishing to be deprived of the King's society, she agreed with him that whenever her husband went to his country-house she would give him notice of it. He might then visit her in safety, and with such secrecy that her honor, which she regarded more than her conscience, would not suffer.[*]

---

bequeathing his Italian possessions to Ferdinand, Duke of Calabria, his natural son by a Spanish beauty named Margaret de Hijar. It may be added that Brantôme makes a passing allusion to this tale of the *Heptameron* in his *Vies des Dames Galantes* (Disc, i.), styling it "a very fine one." — L. and Ed.

[*] Meaning that he employed his sovereign authority for the accomplishment of his amorous desires. — M.

[*] The edition of 1558 is here followed, the MSS. being rather obscure. — M.

Having this hope, the lady continued of very cheerful mind, and when her husband arrived she welcomed him so heartily that, even had he been told that the King had sought her in his absence, he would have had no suspicion. In course of time, however, the flame, that is so difficult of concealment, began to show itself, and the husband, having a strong inkling of the truth, kept good watch, by which means he was well-nigh convinced. Nevertheless, as he feared that the man who wronged him would treat him still worse if he appeared to notice it, he resolved to dissemble, holding it better to live in trouble than to risk his life for a woman who had ceased to love him.

In his vexation of spirit, however, he resolved, if he could, to retort upon the King, and knowing that women, especially such as are of lofty and honorable minds, are more moved by resentment than by love, he made bold one day while speaking with the Queen* to tell her that it moved his pity to see her so little loved by the King.

The Queen, who had heard of the affection that existed between the King and the gentleman's wife, replied —

"I cannot have both honor and pleasure together. I well know that I have the honor whilst another has the pleasure; and in the same way she who has the pleasure has not the honor that is mine."

---

* This was Mary (daughter of Henry III of Castile), who was married to King Alfonso at Valencia on June 29, 1415. Juan de Mariana, the Spanish historian, records that the ceremony was celebrated with signal pomp by the schismatical Pope Benedict XIII. The bride brought her husband a dowry of 200,000 ducats, and also various territorial possessions. The marriage, however, was not a happy one, on account of Alfonso's licentious disposition, and the Queen is said to have strangled one of his mistresses, Margaret de Hijar, in a fit of jealousy. Alfonso, to escape from his wife's interference, turned his attention to foreign expeditions. According to the authors of *L'Art de Vérifier les Dates,* Queen Mary never once set foot in Italy, and this statement is borne out by Mariana, who shows that whilst Alfonso was reigning in Naples his wife governed the kingdom of Aragon, making war and signing truces and treaties of peace with Castile. In the *Heptameron,* therefore, Margaret departs from historical accuracy when she represents the Queen as residing at Naples with her husband. Moreover, judging by the date of Mary's marriage, she could no longer have been young when Alfonso secured the Neapolitan throne. It is to be presumed that the Queen of Navarre designedly changed the date of her story, and that the incidents referred to really occurred in Spain prior to Alfonso's departure for Italy. There is no mention of Mary in her husband's will, a remarkable document which is still extant. A letter written to her by Pope Calixtus II shows that late in life the King was desirous of repudiating her to marry an Italian mistress named Lucretia Alania. The latter repaired to Rome to negotiate the affair, but the Pope refused to treat with her, and wrote to Mary saying that she must be prudent, but that he would not dissolve the marriage, lest God should punish him for participating in so great a crime. Mary died a few months after her husband in 1458, and was buried in a convent at Valencia. — L. and Ed.

Thereupon the gentleman, who understood full well at whom these words were aimed, replied —

"Madam, honor is inborn with you, for your lineage is such that no title, whether of queen or empress, could be an increase of nobility; yet your beauty, grace, and virtue are well deserving of pleasure, and she who robs you of what is yours does a greater wrong to herself than to you, seeing that for a glory which is turned to her shame, she loses as much pleasure as you or any lady in the realm could enjoy. I can truly tell you, madam, that were the King to lay aside his crown, he would not possess any advantage over me in satisfying a lady; nay, I am sure that to content one so worthy as yourself he would indeed be pleased to change his temperament for mine."

The Queen laughed and replied —

"The King may be of a less vigorous temperament than you, yet the love he bears me contents me well, and I prefer it to any other."

"Madam," said the gentleman, "if that were so, I should have no pity for you. I feel sure that you would be well pleased if the like of your own virtuous love were found in the King's heart; but God has withheld this from you in order that, not finding what you desire in your husband, you may not make him your god on earth."

"I confess to you," said the Queen, "that the love I bear him is so great that the like could not be found in any other heart but mine."

"Pardon me, madam," said the gentleman; "you have not fathomed the love of every heart. I will be so bold as to tell you that you are loved by one whose love is so great and measureless that your own is as nothing beside it. The more he perceives that the King's love fails you, the more does his own wax and increase, in such wise that, were it your pleasure, you might be recompensed for all you have lost."

The Queen began to perceive, both from these words and from the gentleman's countenance, that what he said came from the depth of his heart. She remembered also that for a long time he had so zealously sought to do her service that he had fallen into sadness. She had hitherto deemed this to be on account of his wife, but now she was firmly of belief that it was for love of herself. Moreover, the very quality of love, which compels itself to be recognized when it is unfeigned, made her feel certain of what had been hidden from everyone. As she looked at the gentleman, who was far more worthy of being loved than her husband, she reflected that he was forsaken by his wife, as she herself was by the King; and then, beset by vexation and jealousy against her husband, as well as moved by the love of the gentleman, she began with sighs and tearful eyes to say —

"Ah me! shall revenge prevail with me where love has been of no avail?"

The gentleman, who understood what these words meant, replied —

"Vengeance, madam, is sweet when in place of slaying an enemy it gives life to a true lover.* Methinks it is time that truth should cause you to abandon the foolish love you bear to one who loves you not, and that a just and reasonable love should banish fear, which cannot dwell in a noble and virtuous heart. Come, madam, let us set aside the greatness of your station and consider that, of all men and women in the world, we are the most deceived, betrayed, and bemocked by those whom we have most truly loved. Let us avenge ourselves, madam, not so much to requite them in the way they deserve as to satisfy that love which, for my own part, I cannot continue to endure and live. And I think that, unless your heart be harder than flint or diamond, you cannot but feel some spark from the fires which only increase the more I seek to conceal them. If pity for me, who am dying of love for you, does not move you to love me, at least pity for yourself should do so. You are so perfect that you deserve to win the heart of every honorable man in the world, yet you are contemned and forsaken by him for whose sake you have scorned all others."

On hearing these words the Queen was so greatly moved that, for fear of showing in her countenance the trouble of her mind, she took the gentleman's arm and went forth into a garden that was close to her apartment. There she walked to and fro for a long time without being able to say a word to him. The gentleman saw that she was half won, and when they were at the end of the path, where none could see them, he made a very full declaration of the love which he had so long hidden from her. They found that they were of one mind in the matter, and enacted† the vengeance which they were no longer able to forego. Moreover, they there agreed that whenever the husband went into the country, and the King left the castle to visit the wife in the town, the gentleman should always return and come to the castle to see the Queen. Thus, the deceivers being themselves deceived, all four would share in the pleasures that two of them had thought to keep to themselves.

---

* The above sentence being omitted in the MS. followed in this edition, it has been supplied from MS. No. 1520 in the Bibliothèque Nationale. — L.

† This expression has allusion to the mysteries or religious plays so frequently performed in the fifteenth and sixteenth centuries. The Mystery of Vengeance, which depicted the misfortunes which fell upon those who had taken part in the crucifixion of Jesus Christ, such as Pontius Pilate, &c, and ended by the capture and destruction of Jerusalem, properly came after the Mysteries of the Passion and the Resurrection. — L.

When the agreement had been made, the Queen returned to her apartment and the gentleman to his house, both being so well pleased that they had forgotten all their former troubles. The jealousy they had previously felt at the King's visits to the lady was now changed to desire, so that the gentleman went oftener than usual to his house in the country, which was only half a league distant. As soon as the King was advised of his departure, he never failed to go and see the lady; and the gentleman, when night was come, betook himself to the castle to the Queen, where he did duty as the King's lieutenant, and so secretly that none ever discovered it.

This manner of life lasted for a long time; but as the King was a person of public condition, he could not conceal his love sufficiently well to prevent it from coming at length to the knowledge of everyone; and all honorable people felt great pity for the gentleman, though divers malicious youths were wont to deride him by making horns at him behind his back. But he knew of their derision, and it gave him great pleasure, so that he came to think as highly of his horns as of the King's crown.

One day, however, the King and the gentleman's wife, noticing a stag's head that was set up in the gentleman's house, could not refrain in his presence from laughing and saying that the head was suited to the house. Soon afterwards the gentleman, who was no less spirited than the King, caused the following words to be written over the stag's head: —

"Io porto le corna, ciascun lo vede, Ma tal le porta che no lo crede."*

When the King came again to the house, he observed these lines newly written, and inquired their meaning of the gentleman, who said —

"If the King's secret be hidden from the subject, it is not fitting that the subject's secret should be revealed to the King. Be content with knowing that those who wear horns do not always have their caps raised from their heads. Some horns are so soft that they never uncap one, and especially are they light to him who thinks he has them not."

The King perceived by these words that the gentleman knew something of his own behavior, but he never had any suspicion of the love between him and the Queen; for the more pleased the latter was with the life led by her husband, the more did she feign to be distressed by it. And so on either side they lived in this love, until at last old age took them in hand.

---

* "All men may see the horns I've got, But one wears horns and knows it not."

"Here, ladies, is a story by which you may be guided, for, as I willingly confess, it shows you that when your husbands give you bucks' horns you can give them stags' horns in return."

"I am quite sure, Saffredent," began Ennasuite laughing, "that if you still love as ardently as you were formerly wont to do, you would submit to horns as big as oak trees if only you might repay them as you pleased. However, now that your hair is growing grey, it is time to leave your desires in peace."

"Fair lady," said Saffredent, "though I be robbed of hope by the woman I love, and of ardor by old age, yet it lies not in my power to weaken my inclination. Since you have rebuked me for so honorable a desire, I give you my vote for the telling of the fourth tale, that we may see whether you can bring forward some example to refute me."

During this converse one of the ladies fell to laughing heartily, knowing that she who took Saffredent's words to herself was not so loved by him that he would have suffered horns, shame, or wrong for her sake. When Saffredent perceived that the lady who laughed understood him, he was well satisfied and became silent, so that Ennasuite might begin; which she did as follows —

"In order, ladies, that Saffredent and the rest of the company may know that all ladies are not like the Queen he has spoken of, and that all foolhardy and venturesome men do not compass their ends, I will tell you a story in which I will acquaint you with the opinion of a lady who deemed the vexation of failure in love to be harder of endurance than death itself. However, I shall give no names, because the events are so fresh in people's minds that I should fear to offend some who are near of kin."

Tale IV

*A young gentleman sought to discover whether the offer of an honorable love would be displeasing to his master's sister, a lady of the most illustrious lineage in Flanders, who had been twice widowed, and was a woman of muck spirit. Meeting with a reply contrary to his desires, he attempted to possess her by force; but she resisted him successfully, and by the advice of her lady of honor, without seeming to take notice of his designs and efforts, gradually ceased to regard him with the favor with which she had been wont to treat him. Thus, by his foolhardy presumption, he lost the honorable and habitual companionship which, more than others, he had had with her.**

*T*here lived in the land of Flanders a lady of such high lineage, that none more illustrious could be found. She was a widow, both her first and second husbands being dead, and she had no children living. During her widowhood she lived in retirement with her brother, by whom she was greatly loved, and who was a very great lord and married to the daughter of a King. This young Prince was a man much given to pleasure, fond of hunting, pastimes, and women, as his youth inclined him. He had a wife, however, who was of a very froward disposition,† and found no pleasure in her husband's pursuits; wherefore this Lord always took his sister along with his wife, for she was a most joyous and pleasant companion, and withal a discreet and honorable woman.

In this Lord's household there was a gentleman who, for stature, comeliness, and grace, surpassed all his fellows. This gentleman,‡ per-

---

* This story is historical, and the incidents must have occurred between 1520 and 1525. — L.

† The young prince here mentioned is Francis I, who at this period was between twenty-five and thirty years old. The froward wife is Claude of France (daughter of Louis XII and Anne of Brittany), whom Francis married in 1514, and who died of consumption at Blois ten years later, while the King was on his way to conquer Milan. (See the Memoir of Margaret, pp. xxvi. and xxxv.) — Ed.

‡ According to Brantôme, the Lady of Flanders, the young Prince's sister, was Queen Margaret herself, and the gentleman who paid court to her was William Gouffier,

ceiving that his master's sister was of merry mood and always ready for a laugh, was minded to try whether the offer of an honorable love would be displeasing to her.

He made this offer, but the answer that he received from her was contrary to his desires. However, although her reply was such as beseemed a Princess and a woman of true virtue, she readily pardoned his hardihood for the sake of his comeliness and breeding, and let him know that she bore him no ill-will for what he had said. But she charged him never to speak to her after that fashion again; and this he promised, that he might not lose the pleasure and honor of her conversation. Nevertheless, as time went on, his love so increased that he forgot the promise he had made. He did not, however, risk further trial of words, for he had learned by experience, and much against his will, what virtuous replies she was able to make. But he reflected that if he could take her somewhere at a disadvantage, she, being a widow, young, lusty, and of a lively humor, would perchance take pity on him and on herself.

To compass his ends, he told his master that excellent hunting was to be had in the neighborhood of his house, and that if it pleased him to repair thither and hunt three or four stags in the month of May, he could have no finer sport. The Lord granted the gentleman's request, as much for the affection he bore him as for the pleasure of the chase, and repaired to his house, which was as handsome and as fairly ordered as that of the richest gentleman in the land.

The Lord and his Lady were lodged on one side of the house, and she whom the gentleman loved more than himself on the other. Her apartment was so well arranged, tapestried above and matted below,* that it was impossible to perceive a trapdoor which was by the side of

---

Lord of Bonnivet, of Crevecoeur, Thois, and Querdes, and also a favorite of Francis I, with whom he was brought up, and by whom he was employed in all the great enterprises of the time. Bonnivet became Admiral of France in 1517, and two years later he was created governor of Dauphiné, and guardian of the Dauphin's person. He negotiated the peace and alliance with Henry VIII, and arranged all the preliminaries of the interview known as the Field of the Cloth of Gold (1520). In 1521, says Anselme in his *Histoire Généalogique*, Bonnivet became governor of Guienne, commanded the army sent to Navarre, and captured Fontarabia. In 1524 he was dispatched to Italy as lieutenant-general, and besieged Milan, but was repeatedly repulsed, and finally fell back on the Ticino. He was killed at Pavia (February 24, 1525), and was largely responsible for that disastrous defeat, having urged Francis I to give battle, contrary to the advice of the more experienced captains. Bonnivet, as mentioned by Queen Margaret in this story, had the reputation of being one of the handsomest men of his time. — L.

*   In most palaces and castles at this period the walls were covered with tapestry and the floors with matting. This remark is necessary to enable one to understand Bonnivet's stratagem. — D.

her bed, and which opened into a room beneath, that was occupied by the gentleman's mother.*

She being an old lady, somewhat troubled by rheum, and fearful lest the cough she had should disturb the Princess, made exchange of chambers with her son. In the evening this old lady was wont to bring sweetmeats to the Princess for her collation,† at which the gentleman was present; and being greatly beloved by her brother and intimate with him, he was also suffered to be present when she rose in the morning and when she retired to bed, on which occasions he always found reasons for an increase of his affection.

Thus it came to pass that one evening he made the Princess stay up very late, until at last, being desirous of sleep, she bade him leave her. He then went to his own room, and there put on the handsomest and best-scented shirt he had, and a nightcap so well adorned that nothing was lacking in it. It seemed, to him, as he looked at himself in his mirror, that no lady in the world could deny herself to one of his comeliness and grace. He therefore promised himself a happy issue to his enterprise, and so lay down on his bed, where in his desire and sure hope of exchanging it for one more honorable and pleasant, he looked to make no very long stay.

As soon as he had dismissed all his attendants he rose to fasten the door after them; and for a long time he listened to hear whether there were any sound in the room of the Princess, which was above his own. When he had made sure that all was quiet, he wished to begin his pleasant task, and little by little let down the trapdoor, which was so excellently wrought, and so well covered with cloth, that it made not the least noise. Then he ascended into the room and came to the bedside of his lady, who was just falling asleep.

Forthwith, having no regard for the duty that he owed his mistress or for the house to which she belonged, he got into bed with her, without entreating her permission or making any kind of ceremony. She felt him in her arms before she knew that he had entered the room; but being strong, she freed herself from his grasp, and fell to striking, biting, and scratching him, demanding the while to know who he was, so that for fear lest she should call out he sought to stop her mouth with the bedclothes. But this he found it impossible to do, for when she saw that he was using all his strength to work her shame she did as much to baffle him. She further called as loudly as she could to her lady of

---

* Philippa de Montmorency, second wife of William Gouffier, Lord of Boissy, who was Bonnivet's father (Anselme's *Histoire Généalogique*, vol. vii. p. 880). — L.

† At that period the collation, as the supper was called, was served at seven in the evening, shortly before the curfew. — B. J.

honor,* who slept in her room; and this old and virtuous woman ran to her mistress in her nightdress.

When the gentleman saw that he was discovered, he was so fearful of being recognized by the lady, that he descended in all haste through his trapdoor; his despair at returning in such an evil plight being no less than his desire and assurance of a gracious reception had previously been. He found his mirror and candle on his table,† and looking at his face, all bleeding from the lady's scratches and bites, whence the blood was trickling over his fine shirt, which had now more blood than gold‡ about it, he said —

"Beauty! now hast thou been rewarded according to thy deserts. By reason of thy vain promises I attempted an impossible undertaking, and one that, instead of increasing my happiness, will perchance double my misfortune. I feel sure that if she knows I made this foolish attempt contrary to the promise I gave her, I shall lose the honorable and accustomed companionship which more than any other I have had with her. And my folly has well deserved this, for if I was to turn my good looks and grace to any account, I ought not to have hidden them in the darkness. I should not have sought to take that chaste body by force, but should have waited in long service and humble patience till love

---

* The lady in question was Blanche de Tournon, daughter of James de Tournon, by Jane de Polignac, and sister of Cardinal de Tournon, Minister of Francis I. She first married Raymond d'Agout, Baron of Sault in Provençe, who died in 1503; and secondly James de Chastillon, Chamberlain to Charles VIII and Louis XII, killed at the siege of Ravenna in 1512. Brantôme states, moreover, that she subsequently married Cardinal John du Bellay. (See Appendix to the'present volume, C.) In this story, Margaret describes the Princess of Flanders as having lost two husbands, with the view of disguising the identity of her heroine. Her own husband (the Duke of Alençon) was still alive; but Madame de Chastillon had twice become a widow, and the Queen, who was well aware of this, designedly ascribed to the Princess the situation of the lady of honor. This story should be compared with the poem "Quatre Dames et Quatre Gentilhommes" in the *Marguerites de la Marguerite.* — F.

† It is not surprising that the mirror should have been lying on the table. Mirrors were for a long time no larger than our modern hand-glasses. That of Mary de' Medici, offered to her by the Republic of Venice, and now in the Galerie d'Apollon at the Louvre, is extremely small, though it has an elaborate frame enriched with precious cameos. Even the mirrors placed by Louis XIV in the celebrated Galerie des Glaces at Versailles were no larger than ordinary windowpanes. — M.

‡ Shirts were then adorned at the collar and in front with gold-thread embroidery, such as is shown in some of Clouet's portraits. In M. de Laborde's *Comptes des Bâtiments du Roi au XVIème Siècle* (vol. ii.) mention is made of "a shirt with gold work," "a shirt with white work," &c.; and also of two beautiful women's chemises in Holland linen "richly worked with gold thread and silk, at the price of six crowns apiece." — M.

had conquered her. Without love, all man's merits and might are of no avail."

Thus he passed the night in tears, regrets, and sorrowings such as I cannot describe; and in the morning, finding his face greatly torn, he feigned grievous sickness and to be unable to endure the light, until the company had left his house.

The lady, who had come off victorious, knew that there was no man at her brother's Court that durst attempt such an enterprise save him who had had the boldness to declare his love to her. She therefore concluded that it was indeed her host, and made search through the room with her lady of honor to discover how he could have entered it. But in this she failed, whereupon she said to her companion in great anger —

"You may be sure that it can have been none other than the lord of this house, and I will make such report of him to my brother in the morning that his head shall bear witness to my chastity."

Seeing her in such wrath, the lady of honor said to her —

"Right glad am I, madam, to find you esteem your honor so highly that, to exalt it, you would not spare the life of a man who, for the love he bears you, has put it to this risk. But it often happens that one lessens what one thinks to increase; wherefore, I pray you, madam, tell me the truth of the whole matter."

When the lady had fully related the business, the lady of honor said to her —

"You assure me that he had nothing from you save only scratches and blows?"

"I do assure you that it was so," said the lady; "and, unless he find a rare surgeon, I am certain his face will bear the marks tomorrow."

"Well, since it is thus, madam," said the lady of honor, "it seems to me that you have more reason to thank God than to think of vengeance; for you may well believe that, since the gentleman had spirit enough to make such an attempt, his grief at having failed will be harder of endurance than any death you could award him. If you desire to be revenged on him, let love and shame do their work; they will torment him more grievously than could you. And if you would speak out for your honor's sake,* beware, madam, lest you fall into a mishap like to his own.

He, instead of obtaining the greatest delight he could imagine, has encountered the gravest vexation any gentleman could endure. So you,

---

* In Boaistuau's edition this passage runs: "Let love and shame do their work, they will know better than you how to torment him; and do this for your honor's sake. Beware," &c. — L.

madam, thinking to exalt your honor, may perchance diminish it. If you make complaint, you will bring to light what is known to none, for you may rest assured that the gentleman on his side will never reveal aught of the matter. And even if my lord, your brother, should do justice to him at your asking, and the poor gentleman should die, yet would it everywhere be noised abroad that he had had his will of you, and most people would say it was unlikely a gentleman would make such an attempt unless the lady had given him great encouragement. You are young and fair; you live gaily with all; and there is no one at Court but has seen the kind treatment you have shown to the gentleman whom you suspect. Hence everyone will believe that if he did this deed it was not without some fault on your side; and your honor, for which you have never had to blush, will be freely questioned wherever the story is related."

On hearing the excellent reasoning of her lady of honor, the Princess perceived that she spoke the truth, and that she herself would, with just cause, be blamed on account of the close friendship which she had always shown towards the gentleman. Accordingly she inquired of her lady of honor what she ought to do.

"Madam," replied the other, "since you are pleased to receive my counsels, having regard for the affection whence they spring, it seems to me you should be glad at heart to think that the most comely and gallant gentleman I have ever seen was not able, whether by love or by force, to turn you from the path of true virtue. For this, madam, you should humble yourself before God, and confess that it was not through your own merit, for many women who have led straighter lives than you have been humiliated by men less worthy of love than he. And you should henceforth be more than ever on your guard against proposals of love; for many have the second time yielded to dangers which on the first occasion they were able to avoid. Be mindful, madam, that love is blind, and that it makes people blind in such wise that the way appears safest just when it is most slippery. Further, madam, it seems to me that you should give no sign of what has befallen you, whether to him or to anyone else, and that if he seeks to say anything on the matter, you should feign not to understand him. In this way you will avoid two dangers, the one of vain-glory in the victory you have won, and the other of recalling things so pleasant to the flesh that at mention of them the chastest can only with difficulty avoid feeling some sparks of the flame, though they strive their utmost to escape them.* Besides this, madam, in order that he may not think he has done anything pleasing

---

* We here follow MS. No. 1520. — L.

in your sight, I am of opinion you should little by little withdraw the friendship you have been in the habit of showing him. In this way he will know how much you scorn his rashness, and how great is your goodness, since, content with the victory that God has given you, you seek no further vengeance upon him. And may God give you grace, madam, to continue in the virtue He has placed in your heart; and, knowing that all good things come from Him, may you love and serve Him better than before."

The Princess determined to abide by the advice of her lady of honor, and then fell asleep with joy as great as was the sadness of her waking lover.

On the morrow, the lord, her brother, wishing to depart, inquired for his host, and was told that he was too ill to bear the light or to hear anyone speak. The Prince was greatly astonished at this, and wished to go and see the gentleman; however, learning that he was asleep, he would not awake him, but left the house without bidding him farewell. He took with him his wife and sister, and the latter, hearing the excuses sent by the gentleman, who would not see the Prince or any of the company before their departure, felt convinced that it was indeed he who had so tormented her, and that he durst not let the marks which she had left upon his face be seen. And although his master frequently sent for him, he did not return to Court until he was quite healed of all his wounds, save only one — namely, that which love and vexation had dealt to his heart.

When he did return, and found himself in presence of his victorious foe, he could not but blush; and such was his confusion, that he who had formerly been the boldest of all the company, was often wholly abashed before her. Accordingly, being now quite certain that her suspicion was true, she estranged herself from him little by little, though not so adroitly that he did not perceive it; but he durst not give any sign for fear of meeting with something still worse, and so he kept his love concealed, patiently enduring the disgrace he had so well deserved.*

"This, ladies, is a story which should be a warning to those who would grasp at what does not belong to them, and which, further, should strengthen the hearts of ladies, since it shows the virtue of this young Princess, and the good sense of her lady of honor. If the like fortune should befall any among you, the remedy has now been pointed out."

"It seems to me," said Hircan, "that the tall gentleman of whom you have told us was so lacking in spirit as to be unworthy of being

---

* This story is referred to by Brantôme, both in his *Vies des Homines illustres et grands Capitaines français,* and in his *Vies des Dames galantes.* See Appendix to the present volume (C.).

remembered. With such an opportunity as that, he ought not to have suffered anyone, old or young, to baffle him in his enterprise. It must be said, also, that his heart was not entirely filled with love, seeing that fear of death and shame found place within it."

"And what," replied Nomerfide, "could the poor gentleman have done with two women against him?"

"He ought to have killed the old one," said Hircan, "and when the young one found herself without assistance she would have been already half subdued."

"To have killed her!" said Nomerfide. "Then you would turn a lover into a murderer? Since such is your opinion, it would indeed be a fearful thing to fall into your hands."

"If I had gone so far," said Hircan, "I should have held it dishonorable not to achieve my purpose."

Then said Geburon —

"You think it strange that a Princess, bred in all honor, should prove difficult of capture to one man. You should then be much more astonished at a poor woman who escaped out of the hands of two."

"Geburon," said Ennasuite, "I give my vote to you to tell the fifth tale, for I think you know something concerning this poor woman that will not be displeasing to us."

"Since you have chosen me," said Geburon, "I will tell you a story which I know to be true from having made inquiries concerning it on the spot. By this story you will see that womanly sense and virtue are not in the hearts and heads of Princesses alone, nor love and cunning in such as are most often deemed to possess them."

Tale V

Two Grey Friars, when crossing the river at the haven of Coulon, sought to ravish the boatwoman who was taking them over. She, however, being virtuous and Clever, so beguiled them with words that, whilst promising to grant their request, she deceived them and handed them over to justice. They were then delivered up to their warden to receive such punishment as they deserved.

*A*t the haven of Coulon,* near Nyort, there lived a boatwoman who, day or night, did nothing but convey passengers across the ferry.

Now it chanced that two Grey Friars from Nyort were crossing the river alone with her, and as the passage is one of the longest in France, they began to make love to her, that she might not feel dull by the way. She returned them the answer that was due; but they, being neither fatigued by their journeying, nor cooled by the water, nor put to shame by her refusal, determined to take her by force, and, if she clamored, to throw her into the river. She, however, was as virtuous and clever as they were gross and wicked, and said to them —

"I am not so ill-disposed as I seem to be, but I pray you grant me two requests. You shall then see that I am more ready to give than you are to ask."

The friars swore to her by their good St. Francis that she could ask nothing that they would not grant in order to have what they desired of her.

"First of all," she said, "I require you both to promise on oath that you will inform no man living of this matter." This they promised right willingly.

"Then," she continued, "I would have you take your pleasure with me one after the other, for it would be too great a shame for me to have

---

* The village of Coulon, in Poitou (department of the Deux-Sèvres), lies within seven miles of Niort, on the Niortaise Sevre, which at this point is extremely wide. — L.

to do with one in presence of the other. Consider which of you will have me first."

They deemed her request a very reasonable one, and the younger friar yielded the first place to the elder. Then, as they were drawing near a little island, she said to the younger one —

"Good father, say your prayers here until I have taken your companion to another island. Then, if he praises me when he comes back, we will leave him here, and go away in turn together."

The younger friar leapt out on to the island to await the return of his comrade, whom the boat-woman took away with her to another island. When they had reached the bank she said to him, pretending the while to fasten her boat to a tree —

"Look, my friend, and see where we can place ourselves."

The good father stepped on to the island to seek for a convenient spot, but no sooner did she see him on land than she struck her foot against the tree and went off with her boat into the open stream, leaving both the good fathers to their deserts, and crying out to them as loudly as she could —

"Wait now, sirs, till the angel of God comes to console you; for you shall have naught that could please you from me today."

The two poor monks, perceiving that they had been deceived, knelt down at the water's edge and besought her not to put them to such shame; and they promised that they would ask nothing of her if she would of her goodness take them to the haven. But, still rowing away, she said to them —

"I should be doubly foolish if, after escaping out of your hands, I were to put myself into them again."

When she had come to the village, she went to call her husband and the ministers of justice that they might go and take these fierce wolves, from whose fangs she had by the grace of God escaped. They set out accompanied by many people, for there was no one, big or little, but wished to share in the pleasure of this chase.

When the poor brethren saw such a large company approaching, they hid themselves each in his island, even as Adam did when he perceived his nakedness in the presence of God.* Shame set their sin clearly before them, and the fear of punishment made them tremble so that they were half dead. Nevertheless, they were taken prisoners amid the mockings and hootings of men and women.

Some said, "These good fathers preach chastity to us and then rob our wives of theirs."†

---

* See *Genesis* iii. 8-10.

† The editions of 1558 and 1560 here contain this additional phrase: "They do not

Others said, "They are like unto whited sepulchers, which indeed appear beautiful outward, but are within full of dead men's bones and uncleanness."* Then another voice cried, "By their fruits shall ye know what manner of trees they are."†

You may be sure that all the passages in the Gospel condemning hypocrites were brought forward against the unhappy prisoners, who were, however, rescued and delivered by their Warden,‡ who came in all haste to claim them, assuring the ministers of justice that he would visit them with a greater punishment than laymen would venture to inflict, and that they should make reparation by saying as many masses and prayers as might be required. The judge granted the Warden's request and gave the prisoners up to him; and the Warden, who was an upright man, so dealt with them that they never afterwards crossed a river without making the sign of the cross and recommending themselves to God.[1]

"I pray you, ladies, consider, since this poor boatwoman had the wit to deceive two such evil men, what should be done by those who have read of and witnessed so many fair examples, and who have had the goodness of virtuous ladies ever before their eyes? Indeed, the virtue of well-bred women is not so much to be called virtue as habit. It is in the women who know nothing, who hear scarcely two good sermons during the whole year, who have no leisure to think of aught save the gaining of their miserable livelihood, and who nevertheless jealously guard their chastity, hard-pressed as they may be[2] it is in such women as these that one discovers the virtue that is natural to the heart. Where man's wit and might are smallest, there the Spirit of God performs the greatest work. And unhappy indeed is the lady who keeps not close ward over the treasure which brings her so much honor if it be well guarded, and so much shame if it be neglected."

"It seems to me, Geburon," said Longarine, "that there is no great virtue in refusing a Grey Friar, and that it would rather be impossible to love one."

---

dare to touch money with bare hands, and yet they willingly finger the thighs of our wives, which are more dangerous." — L.

* St. Matthew xxiii. 27.

† "For every tree is known by his own fruit." — St. Luke vi. 45.

‡ The Father Superior of the Grey Friars was called the Warden. — B.J.

[1] Henry Etienne quotes this story in his *Apologie pour Hérodote*, and praises the Queen for thus denouncing the evil practices of the friars. — F.

[2] Boaistuau's edition of 1558 here contains the following interpolation: "As should be done by those who, having their lives provided for, have no occupation save that of studying Holy Writ, listening to sermons and preaching, and exerting themselves to act virtuously in all things." — L.

"Longarine," replied Geburon, "they who are not accustomed to such lovers as yours do by no means despise the Grey Friars, for the latter are as handsome and as strong as we are, and they are readier and fresher also, for we are worn-out with our service. Moreover, they talk like angels and are as importunate as the devil, so that such women as have never seen other robes than their coarse drugget ones,* are truly virtuous when they escape out of their hands."

"In faith," said Nomerfide, in a loud voice, "you may say what you like, but I would rather be thrown into the river than lie with a Grey Friar."

"So you can swim well?" said Oisille, laughing.

Nomerfide took this question in bad part, for she thought that she was esteemed by Oisille less highly than she desired. Accordingly she answered in anger —

"There are some who have refused more agreeable men than Grey Friars without blowing a trumpet about it."

Oisille laughed to see her so wrathful, and said to her —

"Still less do they beat a drum about what they have done and granted."

"I see," said Geburon, "that Nomerfide wishes to speak. I therefore give her my vote that she may relieve her heart in telling us some excellent story."

"What has just been said," replied Nomerfide, "touches me so little that it affords me neither pleasure nor pain. However, since I have your vote, I pray you listen to me whilst I show that, although one woman used cunning for a good purpose, others have been crafty for evil's sake. Since we have sworn to tell the truth I will not hide it, for just as the boatwoman's virtue brings no honor to other women unless they follow her example, so the vice of another cannot disgrace her. Wherefore, listen."

---

* Meaning who have never seen gallants in gay apparel. — Ed.

Tale VI

*An old one-eyed valet in the service of the Duke of Alençon being advised
that his wife was in love with a young man, desired to know the truth, and
feigned to go away into the country for a few days. He returned, however, so
suddenly that his wife, on whom he was keeping watch, perceived how
matters stood, and whilst thinking to deceive her, he was himself deceived.*

*T*here was in the service of Charles, last Duke of Alençon, an old
valet who had lost an eye, and who was married to a wife much younger
than himself. Now, since his master and mistress liked him as well as
any man of his condition that was in their service, he was not able to
visit his wife as often as he could have wished. Owing to this she so far
forgot her honor and conscience as to fall in love with a young man,
and the affair being at last noised abroad, the husband heard of it. He
could not believe it, however, on account of the many notable tokens
of love that were shown him by his wife.

Nevertheless, he one day determined to put the matter to the test,
and to take revenge, if he were able, on the woman who had put him
to such shame. For this purpose he pretended to go away to a place a
short distance off for the space of two or three days.

As soon as he was gone, his wife sent for her lover, but he had not
been with her for half-an-hour when the husband arrived and knocked
loudly at the door. The wife well knew who it was and told her lover,
who was so greatly confounded that he would fain have been in his
mother's womb, and cursed both his mistress and the love that had
brought him into such peril. However, she bade him fear nothing, for
she would devise a means to get him away without harm or shame to
him, and she told him to dress himself as quickly as he could. All this
time the husband was knocking at the door and calling to his wife at
the top of his voice; but she feigned not to recognize him, and cried
out to the people of the house —

"Why do you not get up and silence those who are making such a clamor at the door? Is this an hour to come to the houses of honest folk? If my husband were here he would soon make them desist."

On hearing his wife's voice the husband called to her as loudly as he could —

"Wife, open the door. Are you going to keep me waiting here till morning?"

Then, when she saw that her lover was ready to set forth, she opened the door.

"Oh, husband!" she began, "how glad I am that you are come. I have just had a wonderful dream, and was so pleased that I never before knew such delight, for it seemed to me that you had recovered the sight of your eye."*

Then, embracing and kissing him, she took him by the head and covering his good eye with one hand, she asked him —

"Do you not see better than you did before?"

At that moment, whilst he saw not a whit, she made her lover sally forth. The husband immediately suspected the trick, and said to her —

"'Fore God, wife, I will keep watch on you no more, for in thinking to deceive you, I have myself met with the cunningest deception that ever was devised. May God mend you, for it is beyond the power of man to put a stop to the maliciousness of a woman, unless by killing her outright. However, since the fair treatment I have accorded you has availed nothing for your amendment, perchance the scorn I shall henceforward hold you in will serve as a punishment."

So saying he went away, leaving his wife in great distress. Nevertheless by the intercession of his friends and her own excuses and tears, he was persuaded to return to her again.†

---

* This is taken from No. xvi. of the *Cent Nouvelles Nouvelles,* in which the wife exclaims: "Verily, at the very moment when you knocked, my lord, I was greatly occupied with a dream about you." — "And what was it, sweetheart?" asks the husband. — "By my faith, my lord," replies the wife, "it really seemed to me that you were come back, that you were speaking to me, and that you saw as clearly with one eye as with the other." — Ed.

† Although Queen Margaret ascribes the foregoing adventure to one of the officers of her husband's household, and declares that the narrative is quite true, the same subject had been dealt with by most of the old story-tellers prior to her time, and Deslongchamps points out the same incidents even in the early Hindu fables (see the *Pantcha Tantra,* book I, fable vi.). A similar tale is to be found in the *Gesta Romanorum* (cap. cxxii.), in the *fabliaux* collected by Legrand d'Aussy (vol. iv., "De la mauvaise femme"), in P. Alphonse's *Disciplina Clericalis* (fab. vii.), in the *Decameron* (day vii., story vi.), and in the *Cent Nouvelles Nouvelles* (story xvi.). Imitations are also to be found in Bandello (part i., story xxiii.), Malespini (story xliv.), Sansovino (*Cento Novelle*), Sabadino (*Novelle*), Etienne (*Apologiepour Hérodote,* ch. xv.), De la

"By this tale, ladies, you may see how quick and crafty a woman is in escaping from danger. And if her wit be quick to discover the means of concealing a bad deed, it would, in my belief, be yet more subtle in avoiding evil or in doing good; for I have always heard it said that wit to do well is ever the stronger."

"You may talk of your cunning as much as you please," said Hircan, "but my opinion is that had the same fortune befallen you, you could not have concealed the truth."

"I had as lief you deemed me the most foolish woman on earth," she replied.

"I do not say that," answered Hircan, "but I think you more likely to be confounded by slander than to devise some cunning means to silence it."

"You think," said Nomerfide, "that everyone is like you, who would use one slander for the patching of another; but there is danger lest the patch impair what it patches and the foundation be so overladen that all be destroyed. However, if you think that the subtlety, of which all believe you to be fully possessed, is greater than that found in women, I yield place to you to tell the seventh story; and, if you bring yourself forward as the hero, I doubt not that we shall hear wickedness enough."

"I am not here," replied Hircan, "to make myself out worse than I am; there are some who do that rather more than is to my liking."

So saying he looked at his wife, who quickly said —

"Do not fear to tell the truth on my account. I can more easily bear to hear you relate your crafty tricks than to see them played before my eyes, though none of them could lessen the love I bear you."

"For that reason," replied Hircan, "I make no complaint of all the false opinions you have had of me. And so, since we understand each other, there will be more security for the future. Yet I am not so foolish as to relate a story of myself, the truth of which might be vexatious to you. I will tell you one of a gentleman who was among my dearest friends."

Monnoye (vol. ii.), D'Ouville (*Contes,* vol. ii.), &c. — L. & B. J.

Tale VII

By the craft and subtlety of a merchant an old woman was deceived and the honor of her daughter saved.

*I*n the city of Paris there lived a merchant who was in love with a young girl of his neighborhood, or, to speak more truly, she was more in love with him than he with her. For the show he made to her of love and devotion was but to conceal a loftier and more honorable passion. However, she suffered herself to be deceived, and loved him so much that she had quite forgotten the way to refuse.

After the merchant had long taken trouble to go where he could see her, he at last made her come whithersoever it pleased himself. Her mother discovered this, and being a very virtuous woman, she forbade her daughter ever to speak to the merchant on pain of being sent to a nunnery. But the girl, whose love for the merchant was greater than her fear of her mother, went after him more than ever.

It happened one day, when she was in a closet all alone, the merchant came in to her, and finding himself in a place convenient for the purpose, fell to conversing with her as privily as was possible. But a maid-servant, who had seen him go in, ran and told the mother, who betook herself thither in great wrath. When the girl heard her coming, she said, weeping, to the merchant — "Alas! sweetheart, the love that I bear you will now cost me dear. Here comes my mother, who will know for certain what she has always feared and suspected."

The merchant, who was not a bit confused by this accident, straightway left the girl and went to meet the mother. Stretching out his arms, he hugged her with all his might, and, with the same ardor with which he had begun to entertain the daughter, threw the poor old woman on to a small bed. She was so taken aback at being thus treated that she could find nothing to say but — "What do you want? Are you dreaming?"

For all that he ceased not to press her as closely as if she had been the fairest maiden in the world, and had she not cried out so loudly that her serving-men and women came to her aid, she would have gone by the same road as she feared her daughter was treading.

However, the servants dragged the poor old woman by main force out of the merchant's arms, and she never knew for what reason he had thus used her. Meanwhile, her daughter took refuge in a house hard by where a wedding was going on. Since then she and the merchant have ofttimes laughed together at the expense of the old woman, who was never any the wiser.

"By this story, ladies, you may see how, by the subtlety of a man, an old woman was deceived and the honor of a young one saved. Anyone who would give the names, or had seen the merchant's face and the consternation of the old woman, would have a very tender conscience to hold from laughing. It is sufficient for me to prove to you by this story that a man's wit is as prompt and as helpful at a pinch as a woman's, and thus to show you, ladies, that you need not fear to fall into men's hands. If your own wit should fail you, you will find theirs prepared to shield your honor."

"In truth, Hircan," said Longarine, "I grant that the tale is a very pleasant one and the wit great, but the example is not such as maids should follow. I readily believe there are some whom you would fain have approve it, but you are not so foolish as to wish that your wife, or her whose honor you set higher than her pleasure,* should play such a game. I believe there is none who would watch them more closely or shield them more readily than you."

"By my conscience," said Hircan, "if she whom you mention had done such a thing, and I knew nothing about it, I should think nonetheless of her. For all I know, someone may have played as good a trick on me; however, knowing nothing, I am unconcerned."

At this Parlamente could not refrain from saying —

"A wicked man cannot but be suspicious; happy are those who give no occasion for suspicion."

"I have never seen a great fire from which there came no smoke," said Longarine, "but I have often seen smoke where there was no fire. The wicked are as suspicious when there is no mischief as when there is."

"Truly, Longarine," Hircan forthwith rejoined, "you have spoken so well in support of the honor of ladies wrongfully suspected, that I give you my vote to tell the eighth tale. I hope, however, that you will not

---

* M. Frank, adopting the generally received opinion that Hircan is King Henry of Navarre, believes this to be an allusion to one of the King's sisters — Ann, who married the Count of Estrac, or Isabel, who married M. de Rohan — but it is more likely that Henry's daughter, Jane d'Albret, is the person referred to. — Ed.

make us weep, as Madame Oisille did, by too much praise of virtuous women."

At this Longarine laughed heartily, and thus began: — "You want me to make you laugh, as is my wont, but it shall not be at women's expense. I will show you, however, how easy it is to deceive them when they are inclined to be jealous and esteem themselves clever enough to deceive their husbands."

APPENDIX

A. (Prologue)

The dedication with which Anthony Le Maçon prefaces his translation of Boccaccio contains several curious passages. In it Margaret is styled "the most high and most illustrious Princess Margaret of France, only sister of the King, Queen of Navarre, Duchess of Alençon and of Berry;" while the author describes himself as "Master Anthoine Le Maçon, Councilor of the King, Receiver General of his finances in Burgundy, and very humble secretary to this Queen." He then proceeds to say: —

"You remember, my lady, the time when you made a stay of four or five months in Paris, during which you commanded me, seeing that I had freshly arrived from Florence, where I had sojourned during an entire year, to read to you certain stories of the *Decameron* of Boccaccio, after which it pleased you to command me to translate the whole book into our French language, assuring me that it would be found beautiful and entertaining. I then made you reply that I felt my powers were too weak to undertake such a work. . . . My principal and most reasonable excuse was the knowledge that I had of myself, being a native of the land of Dauphiné, where the maternal language is too far removed from good French. . . . However, it did not please you to accept any of my excuses, and you showed me that it was not fitting that the Tuscans should be so mistaken as to believe that their Boccaccio could not be rendered in our language as well as it is in theirs, ours having become so rich and so copious since the accession of the King, your brother, to the crown, that nothing has ever been written in any language that could not be expressed in this; and thus your will still was that I should translate it (the *Decameron*) when I had the leisure to do so. Seeing this and desiring, throughout my life, to do, if I can, even more than is possible to obey you, I began some time afterwards to translate one of the said stories, then two, then three, and finally to the number of ten or twelve, the best that I could choose, which I afterwards showed as much to people of the Tuscan nation as to people of ours, who all made me believe that the stories were, if not perfectly, at least very faithfully translated. Wherefore, allowing myself to be thus pleasantly deceived, if deceit there was, I have since set myself to begin the translation at one end and to finish it at the other. . . ."

This dedicatory preface is followed by an epistle, written in Italian by Emilio Ferretti, and dated from Lyons, May I, 1545; and by a notice to the reader signed by Etienne Rosset, the bookseller, who in the King's license, dated from St. Germain-en-Laye, Nov. 2, 1544, is described as "Rosset called the Mower, bookseller, residing in Paris, on the bridge of St. Michael, at the sign of the White Rose." The first edition of Le Maçon's translation (1545) was in folio; the subsequent ones of 1548, 1551, and 1553 being in octavo. It should be remembered that Le Maçon's was by no means the first French version of the *Decameron.* Laurent du Premier-Faict had already rendered Boccaccio's masterpiece into French in the reign of Charles VI, but unfortunately his translation, although of a pleasing naïveté, was not at all correct, having been made from a Latin version of the original. Manuscript copies of Laurent's translation were to be found in the royal and most of the princely libraries of the fifteenth century. — Ed.

B. (Tale I)

The letters of remission which at the instance of Henry VIII were granted to Michael de St. Aignan in respect of the murder of James du Mesnil are preserved in the National Archives of France (Register J. 234, No. 191), and after the usual preamble, recite the culprit's petition in these terms: —

"Whereas it appears from the prayer of Michael de St. Aignan, lord of the said place,* that heretofore he for a long time lived and resided in the town of Alençon in honor and good repute; but, to the detriment of his prosperity, life, and conduct there were divers evil-minded and envious persons who by sinister, cunning, and hidden means persecuted him with all the evils, wiles, and deceits that it is possible to conceive, albeit the said suppliant had never caused them displeasure, injury, or detriment; among others, one named James Dumesnil, a young man, to whom the said suppliant had procured all the pleasure and advantages that were in his power, and whom he had customarily admitted to his house, thinking that the said Dumesnil was his loyal friend, and charging his wife and his servants to treat him when he came as though he were his brother; by which means St. Aignan hoped to induce the said Dumesnil to espouse one of his relatives.

"But Dumesnil ill-requited the aforesaid good services and courtesies, and rendering evil for good, as is the practice of iniquity, endeavored to and did cause an estrangement between the said St. Aignan and his wife, who had always lived together in good, great, and perfect affection. And the better to effect his purpose he (Dumesnil) gave the said wife to understand, among other things, that St. Aignan bore her no affec-

---

* This was in all probability the village of St. Aignan on the Sarthe, between Moulins-la-Marche and Bazoches, and about twenty miles from Alençon. The personage here mentioned should not be confounded with Emery de Beauvilliers, whom Francis I created Count of St. Aignan (on the Cher), and whose descendants, many of whom were distinguished generals and diplomatists, became dukes of the same place. — Ed.

tion; that he daily desired her death; that she was mistaken in trusting him; and other evil things not fitting to be repeated, which the wife withstood, enjoining Dumesnil not to use such language again, as should he do so she would repeat it to her husband; but Dumesnil, persevering, on divers occasions when St. Aignan had absented himself, gave the wife of the latter to understand that he (St. Aignan) was dead, devising proofs thereof and conjectures, and thinking that by this means he would win her favor and countenance. But she still resisted him, which seeing, the said Dumesnil gave her to understand that St. Aignan would often absent himself, and that she would be happier if she had a husband who remained with her. And plotting to compass the death of the said St. Aignan, Dumesnil gave her to understand that if she would consent to the death of her husband he would marry her; and, in fact, he promised to marry her. And whereas she still refused to consent, the said Dumesnil found a means to gain a servant woman of the house, who, St. Aignan being absent and his wife in bed, opened the door to Dumesnil, who compelled the said wife to let him lie with her. And thenceforward Dumesnil made divers presents to the servant woman, so that she should poison the said suppliant; and she consented to his face; but at Easter confessed the matter to St. Aignan, entreating his forgiveness, and also saying and declaring it to the neighbors. And the said Dumesnil, knowing that he would incur blame and reproach if the matter were brought forward, seized and abducted the said servant woman in all diligence, and took her away from the town, whereby a scandal was occasioned.

"Moreover, it would appear that the said Dumesnil had been found several times by night watching the gardens and the door in view of slaying St. Aignan, as is notorious in Alençon, by virtue of the admission of the said Dumesnil himself. Whereupon St. Aignan, seeing his wife thus made the subject of scandal by Dumesnil, enjoined him to abstain from coming to his house to see his wife, and to consider the outrage and injury he had already inflicted upon him; declaring moreover that he could endure no more. To which Dumesnil refused to listen, declaring that he would frequent the house in spite of everyone; albeit, in doing so, he might come by his death. Thereupon St. Aignan, being acquainted with the evil obstinacy of Dumesnil and desirous of avoiding greater misfortune, departed from the town of Alençon, and went to reside in the town of Argentan, ten leagues distant, whither he took his wife, thinking that Dumesnil would abstain from coming. Withal he did not abstain, but came several times to the said town of Argentan, and frequented his (St. Aignan's) wife; whereby the people of Argentan were scandalized. And the said St. Aignan endeavored to prevent him from coming, and employed the nurse of his child to remonstrate with Dumesnil, but the latter persevered, saying and declaring that he would kill St. Aignan, and would still go to Argentan, albeit it might cause his death. Insomuch that the said Dumesnil, on the eighth day of this month, departed from Alençon between two and three o'clock in the morning, a suspicious hour, having disguised himself and assumed attire unsuited to his calling, which is that of the law; wearing a Bearnese cloak,* a jacket of white woolen stuff underneath, all torn into strips, with a feathered cap upon his head, and having his face covered. In this wise he arrived at the said town of Argentan, accompanied by two young men, and lodged in the faubourgs at the sign of Notre Dame, and remained there clandestinely from noon till about eleven o'clock in the evening, when he asked the host for the key of the backdoor, so that he might go out on his private affairs, not wishing to be recognized.

"At the said suspicious hour, with his sword at his side,† and dressed and accoutered in the said garments, he started from his lodging with one of the said young men.

"In this wise Dumesnil reached the house of St. Aignan, which he found a means of entering, and gained a closet up above, near the room where the said St. Aignan and his wife slept. St. Aignan was without thought of this, inasmuch as he was ignorant of the enterprise of the said Dumesnil, being in the living room with one Master Thomas Guérin, who had come upon business. Now, as St. Aignan was disposing himself to go to bed, he told one of his servants, named Colas, to bring him his cas‡ and the servant having occasion to go up into a closet in which St. Aignan's wife was sleeping, and in which the said Dumesnil was concealed, the latter, fearing that he might be recognized, suddenly came out with a drawn sword in his hand; whereupon the said Colas cried: 'Help! There is a robber!' And he declared to St. Aignan that he had seen a strange man who did not seem to be there for any good purpose; whereupon St. Aignan said to him: 'One must find out who it is. Is there occasion for anyone to come here at this hour?' Thereupon Colas went after the said personage, whom he found in a little alley near the courtyard behind the house; and the said personage, having suddenly perceived Colas, endeavored to strike him on the body with his

---

* See *ante*, p. 24, note 8.

† The French word is *basion*, which in the sixteenth century was often used to imply a sword; harquebuses and musketoons being termed *basions à feu* by way of distinction. Moreover, it is expressly stated farther on that Dumesnil had a sword. — Ed.

‡ The *en cas* was a kind of light supper provided *in case* one felt hungry at night-time. Most elaborate *en cas*, consisting of several dishes, were frequently provided for the kings of France. — Ed.

weapon; but Colas withstood him and gave him a few blows,* for which reason he cried out 'Help! Murder!' Thereupon St. Aignan arrived, having a sword in his hand; and after him came the said Guérin. St. Aignan, who as yet did not know Dumesnil on account of his disguise, and also because it was wonderfully dark, found him calling out: 'Murder! Confession!' By which cry the said St. Aignan knew him, and was greatly perplexed, astonished, and angered, at seeing his enemy at such an hour in his house, he having been found there, with a weapon, in the closet. And the said St. Aignan recalling to memory the trouble and worry that Dumesnil had caused him, dealt him two or three thrusts in hot anger, and then said to him: 'Hey! Wretch that thou art, what hast brought thee here? Wert thou not content with the wrong thou didst me in coming here previously? I never did thee an ill office.' Whereupon the said Dumesnil said: 'It is true, I have too grievously offended you, and am too wicked; I entreat your pardon.' And thereupon he fell to the ground as if dead; which seeing, the said St. Aignan, realizing the misfortune that had happened, said not a word, but recommended himself to God and withdrew into his room, where he found his wife in bed, she having heard nothing.

"On the night of the said dispute, and a little later, St. Aignan went to see what the said Dumesnil was doing, and finding him in the courtyard dead, he helped to carry him into the stable, being too greatly incensed to act otherwise. And upon the said Colas asking him what should be done with the body, St. Aignan paid no heed to this question, because he was not master of himself; but merely said to Colas that he might do as he thought fit, and that the body might be interred in consecrated ground or placed in the street. After which St. Aignan withdrew into his room and slept with his wife, who had her maids with her. And on the morrow this same Colas declared to St. Aignan that he had taken the said body to be buried, so as to avoid a scandal. To all of which things St. Aignan paid no heed, but on the morrow sent to fetch the two young men in the service of the said Dumesnil, who were at his lodging, and had the horses removed from the said lodging, and gave orders to one of the young men to take them back.

"On account of all which occurrences he (St. Aignan) absented himself, &c, &c, but humbly entreating us, &c, &c. Wherefore we now give to the Bailiffs of Chartres and Caen, or to their Lieutenants, and to each of them severally and to all, &c, &c. Given at Châtelherault, in the month of July, the year of Grace, one thousand five hundred and twenty-six, and the twelfth of our reign.

---

* In the story Margaret asserts that it was Thomas Guérin who attacked Dumesnil. — D.

"Signed: By the King on the report of the Council:
"De Nogent." *Visa: contentor.*
"De Nogent"*

---

* It will be seen that the foregoing petition contains various contradictory statements. The closet, for instance, is at first described as being near the room in which St. Aignan and his wife slept, then it is asserted that the wife slept in the closet, but ultimately the husband is shown joining his wife in the bedchamber, where she had heard nothing. The character of the narrative is proof of its falsity, and Margaret's account of the affair may readily be accepted as the more correct one. – Ed.

C. (Tale IV)

*L*es *Vies des Dames galantes* contains the following passage bearing upon Margaret's 4th Tale. See Lalanne's edition of Brantôme's Works, vol. ix. p. 678 *et sec*.: —

"I have heard a lady of great and ancient rank relate that the late Cardinal du Bellay, whilst a Bishop and Cardinal, married Madame de Chastillon, and died married; and this lady said it in conversing with Monsieur de Manne, a Provençal of the house of Seulal, and Bishop of Frejus, who had attended the said Cardinal during fifteen years at the Court of Rome, and had been one of his private protonotaries. The conversation turning upon the said Cardinal, this lady asked Monsieur de Manne if he (the Cardinal) had ever said and confessed to him that he had been married. It was Monsieur de Manne who was astonished at such a question. He is still alive and can say if I am telling an untruth, for I was there. He replied that he had never heard the matter spoken of either to himself or to others. 'Then it is I who inform you of it,' said she, 'for nothing could be more true but that he was married, and died really married to Madame de Chastillon.'

"I assure you that I laughed heartily, contemplating the astonished countenance of Monsieur de Manne, who was most conscientious and religious, and thought that he had known all the secrets of his late master; but he was as ignorant as a Gibuan as regards that one, which was indeed scandalous on account of the holy rank which he (Cardinal du Bellay) had held.

"This Madame de Chastillon was the widow of the late Monsieur de Chastillon, of whom it was said that he governed the little King Charles VIII, with Bourdillon and Bonneval, who governed the royal blood. He died at Ferrara, where he had been taken to have his wounds dressed, having been wounded at the siege of Ravenna.

"This lady became a widow when very young and beautiful, and on account of her being sensible and virtuous she was elected as lady of honor to the late Queen of Navarre. It was she who gave that fine advice to that lady and great princess, which is recorded in the hundred stories of the said Queen — the story of herself and a gentleman who had slipped into her bed during the night by a trapdoor at the bedside, and who wished to enjoy her, but only obtained by it some fine scratches upon his handsome face. She (the Queen) wishing to complain to her brother, Madame de Chastillon made her that fine remonstrance which will be seen in the story, and gave her that beautiful advice which is one of the finest, most judicious, and most fitting that could be given to avoid scandal: did it come even from a first president of (the Parliament of) Paris. Yet it well showed that the lady was quite as artful and shrewd in such secret matters as she was sensible and prudent; and for this reason there is no need for doubt as to whether she kept her affair with the Cardinal a secret. My grandmother, Madame la Sénéchale of Poitou, had her place after her death, by election of King Francis who chose and elected her, and sent to fetch her even in her house, and gave her with his own hand to the Queen his sister, for he knew her to be a very well-advised and very virtuous lady, but not so shrewd, or artful, or ready-witted in such matters as her predecessor, or married either a second time.

"And if you wish to know to whom the story applies, it is to the Queen of Navarre herself and Admiral de Bonnivet, as I hold it from my late grandmother; and yet it seems to me that the said Queen should not have concealed her name, since the other could not obtain aught from her chastity, but went off in confusion, and since she herself had meant to divulge the matter had it not been for the fine and sensible remonstrance which was made to her by the said lady of honor, Madame de Chastillon. Whoever has read the story will find that she was a lady of honor, and I think that the Cardinal, her said husband, who was one of the best speakers and most learned, eloquent, wise, and shrewd men of his time, must have instilled into her this science of speaking and remonstrating so well."

Brantôme also refers to the story in question in his *Vies des Hommes illustres et grands Capitaines français* (vol. ii. p. 162), wherein he says: —

"There is a tale in the stories of the Queen of Navarre, which speaks of a lord, the favorite of a king, whom he invited with all his court to one of his houses, where he made a trapdoor in his room conducting to the bedside of a great princess, in view of lying with her, as he did, but, as the story relates, he obtained only scratches from her."